DEMON DESIRED

by
Ysadora
Sonderling

Sonderling
Publishing House

For Ben, and the cats, who tried very hard to distract me from finishing this book.
For naps, making life worthwhile.

The Bayton Agency
Demon Desired
Demon Hunted
Demon Enchanted

Stand-Alone
Heaven For a Predator

ISBN eBook: 978-1-7636874-2-4
ISBN Paperback: 978-1-7636874-3-1

First edition published 15th February 2025

Cover design by Fieriz Design.

Prologue

His breath hitched in his throat. The one hunting him was so close. There was a dark pall over the already bleak night, and somewhere within stalked the one pursuing him. The glare of a predator had nagged him all evening, a lingering notion of a threat that he initially tried to laugh off. When in a full pub it was easy to do, surrounded by intoxicated friends and intoxicating women.

Now he was alone.

The street stretched into the gloom; the streetlights unusually absent. Sounds dulled, gone were the usual cars trawling for the girls whose steel heeled stilettos beat out a tattoo of the flesh trade. No bawdy songs or hacking coughs that narrated his usual walk home. Tonight, it had all dissipated into a miasma of fear. He ran for the next alley, waiting for his eyes to adjust to the sudden darkness. There was a scratch, a sigh. A stench to overwhelm the senses. While he had hoped to hide out in this moist alley way, littered with the discarded refuse of a sex and drugs kind of town, it seemed to be already occupied. While the greasy illumination of a streetlight still flowed into the mouth of the alley, it barely penetrated halfway down the first wall. Despite the impenetrable darkness, he knew that there were a great many beings hidden beyond the meagre light. As someone stepped across the mouth of the alley and blocked his light, he knew he was trapped.

'Is this about my...' His final words were cut short with the blade of a knife and many grabbing, rotting hands.

Chapter One

Tessa had never really been one to rely on her sensual nature, but if the time called for it, she could certainly play up on her best visual attributes. She stank of flowery perfume, rouged her cheeks and had even put on sheer pantyhose. The low-cut blouse on the other hand, that was a staple of her usual work attire, along with sky high heels.

Fidgeting on the spot, Tessa began fluffing her already teased out hair, comforting herself mindlessly while she waited for those huge, intricately carved oak double doors to open and the interview that would change her entire life to start. Tessa had been an intern witch with the Agency for four years now, and now her future as a fully-fledged witch, an Agent, depended on how well she could schmooze the lurid, sexist pig in charge of her division. It was well known that he was loathe to promote a woman, although so far, he had shown a distinct weakness for a pretty smile and "lady-like" rose perfume. Now it was Tessa's time to play on that weakness.

The Agency had once had an official name, but it had long fallen into disuse as it didn't really have any competition. They were something of a police force, defending the innocent magickal beings and mundanes, the non-magickal people, from the eviller witches and entities who needed to be... controlled. These were the necromancers, the hex casters, the magickal serial killers. The summoners of violent spirits and creators of foul magickal creatures. These offenders all fell under the Agencies jurisdiction. They were the final word on all crimes of a magickal nature. If a crime was clearly proven, the Agency were freely given the right to be judge, jury and executioner. Such was the fear of the mundane population when it came to magick as a whole.

The Agency was a hierarchical and bureaucratic mess, while holding the reins were the oldest witching families and their incomes. Nepotism was popular, but for all its flaws, the Agency was entirely a necessity.

Interns made very little money, as all the bonuses for a job well done went to their mentors, despite it generally being the interns who had done all the legwork. The intern system was a joke, but it was one of those "bureaucratic system" things that had never progressed from the 1950's. Regardless, Tessa had made it through her various trials and was ready for her final assessment.

Unfortunately, said assessment was the responsibility of the heads of each department. While they had the mentor's notes, the supervisors had the final say of the careers of people they barely knew.

While she should get through on merit alone, a little flirtatious insurance never went astray. She clicked open her compact, hastily powdering her nose and checking her appearance one last time. Not stunning, but she guessed she could pass as a bit of a looker really. Certainly, she had never lived up to the standard that her mother had aspired. With her hair dyed as red as a cheap sports car and a smattering of freckles, Tessa would almost be cute if it weren't for the many tattoos and piercings. Sure, many of the tattoos were of the magickal sigil kind, the traditional markings of her profession, but they were interspersed with plenty of pin up girls, sugar skulls and the occasional XXX poison bottle. Dressing to kill, complete with liberty rolls and swing skirt was the best way to get by when you lived on the edge, in the Bayton city slum.

Nearby a stern throat cleared, breaking Tessa out of her reverie. Sir McAdams was leering over her, probably hoping to catch a better view down her shirt. She snapped her compact shut and threw it in her bag before rising as sensuously as she could, although she felt more akin to a newborn giraffe attempting to stand.

Her sensual efforts must have been at least a little effective, the Sir's eyes were now bugging out of their red, watery rims as his puffy face reddened. It was a repulsive, sweaty mess.

Why was it that all sleazy men seemed to have red watery eyes, she mused as she tottered into the office, *was it because they all stare at anything with a hint of cleavage far too much? Did it cause some kind of permanent damage?*

Distracting herself with such inane thoughts would not help her with what was to come. She had to focus. It was time for a little game of make believe.

Tessa perched on the edge of the offered chair as the Sir hefted his putrid bulk around the desk, ungainly throwing himself down in a blobby heap. His shirt tails poked out of his pants, stained with many past meals wiped from his hands. His tie was the elasticated kind, and had seen too many sweaty board meetings given the way it hung loosely, with elastic long perished. Filthy glasses sat low on his nose and a wet bottom lip hung lower. Sir McAdams was a caricature of a man, the personification of middle management. How he had ever been a field Agent was a popular subject of postulation by the interns. He cleared his throat again, perhaps attempting to look wise, and began to leaf through what Tessa assumed was her employee file.

'Contessa Bale,' he murmured as Tessa flinched. Her mother had big dreams and a poor sense of humour when it came to naming her bouncing blonde bundle of joy. Imagine her disappointment when Tessa became an Agency witch rather than a trophy wife.

She had jumped on the opportunity when the official Agency examiners had come to her school. It was finally a chance at a future which interested her more than the tedium of being a pretty wife to a rich man.

No one expected her to pass, let alone pass with skills that were above the contemporary testable power levels. It was her ticket out of there and she grabbed it with both hands. Who cared that she lived in the slum area of Bayton, that her car barely ran, and the neighbours were less than desirable.

To Tessa that just made them more real. She was eternally thankful to have won the genetic lottery of being born with magickal skills. Sir McAdams coughed again and leafed through a few more papers, to what end she had no clue. Somewhere in the middle-management script was "make them wait."

'Contessa, you are here to be assessed as to whether you are ready to be deemed a fully qualified and registered witch of the Agency are you not?' he said, in a thin voice that was attempting authority but getting lost in the slime. She nodded, before working to get her own voice to resonate with those dulcet tones usually favoured by phone sex line workers and other talented strumpets. It felt foreign on her tongue.

'Yes Sir, if I am worthy...' She almost choked on the effort of forming the words thus, but the quick tug of the collar indicated that her ploy had worked.

'Well Contessa, you appear to have an exemplary record, while working under your mentor your capture or kill rate has been outstanding. The mentor's notes are good, Lady Marique has indicated you handle yourself well with matters both magickal and mundane. No innocent or mundane loss. Yes, yes quite the record.' Tessa fought the need to roll her eyes; thus far the Sir's own eyes had done more wandering of her body than her record. Although, that was the idea.

'I believe I am ready Sir,' she said, batting her eyes, hopefully coquettishly, although the overall effect was probably more comparable to having a seizure. Sir McAdams sniffed, waving a hand idly. Clearly that slight challenge to his authoritarian decision was undesirable.

'I will ascertain that. However, your record is good. We do have more cases than available and competent witches right now so I shall allow you to go through. Hereby you shall be known as Lady Bale, an investigatory witch of the Agency with full powers of the law both magickal and mundane.' With those final words Sir McAdams puffed out his chest with self-importance, magnanimously bestowing this gift of a bigger pay packet and nondescript title. He reached for a red folder from the top of the stack of files that permanently littered his desk.

'You will be honoured to know we have already assigned you a case. The details are in here, something to do with goings on in the area you live I believe. Take it now, any research you need can be done in the Halls. Report to Lady Kirk in order to get your restricted spell items also, along with the witches' sigil.' With one last leer Sir McAdams turned away, reviewing the folder of what Tessa assumed was the next interviewee.

Those simple words and that was it, she was an indoctrinated witch. She muttered a thanks and grabbed the folder, fleeing the sense of being pawed at and undressed with the sweaty pervert's eyes. While she exploited the sleazier men in her life when it was necessary, it didn't make her feel good after the fact. Perhaps a shower in bleach, perhaps some steel wool, perhaps some industrial cleaner, then she would feel more at ease.

The Agency had a rigid hierarchical system, indoctrinated witches were called Sir or Lady to delegate their rank above that of an intern. There were also the Sibyls, who had the dual role of being on hand seers and admin staff, as well as the Elders who had done their duty in the field and survived. The Elders were rather rare, and greatly revered. The Elders were cared for until the day they died at the Agency, such was their value.

The advice of the Elders was greatly sought after by the Agent witches, and the Sibyls often attended the Elders for insight on what they had seen.

This system was both flawed and seamless. Initiation rituals were done when an intern was approved to join the Agency. It was a ritual and legal binding, full of spellwork and paperwork. The actual success rate of interns making it to a full witch was relatively small, although luckily death was rare. It was far more likely that an intern would drop out, something Tessa had considered many times. Her mentor Lady Marique had been stern, and many of the other interns had been terrified of the fierce woman. Tessa had welcomed her nature, as it came with an unconditional support.

Plus, she didn't particularly care for fitting in with her fellow interns. Many had come from the well to do, rich witching families that controlled the Agency, and had the personalities and work ethic to match. Being born to a mundane family, however rich it was, and living in the slum meant that Tessa was a pariah, ostracised from their inner circle-jerk. Her few friends she did have were considered the deviants and weirdoes, those forced to live at the Agency.

The halls of the Agency were busy, so it took Tessa quite a while to squeeze her way through the loiterers and head to Lady Kirk's... repository, for want of a better word. Part storehouse, part tattoo parlour, part impromptu therapy clinic, it was the go-to for all Agency witches, where they got all necessary magickal ingredients for spells or the latest magickal sigil carved into their flesh.

Tessa loved these rooms, where the heady scent of herbs and dried animal parts drifted over the subtle disinfectant used for the tattoo area. Rich wooden shelves of magickal accoutrements and loose herbs at one end, autoclaves and stainless steel at the other. Lady Kirk was not busy for once, keeping a shrewd eye on a few young Sibyls digging through the yarrow and mugwort. She greeted Tessa warmly.

With an open face surrounded by a shock of greying hair, Lady Kirk was agelessly stylish. Her unusual amber eyes were framed by cat-eye glasses. With a fondness for brightly coloured kaftan style dresses, Lady Kirk was a glorious burst of vibrancy in the drab Agency halls. Her prominent tattoos were equally bright, which Tessa loved to see on an older woman. Lady Kirk was all bright smiles and musical laughs.

'You are finally a witch, my dear! Ready for the big wide world?' she said, teasing gently in her soft voice that had always calmed Tessa.

This time the new witch allowed herself the luxury of rolling her eyes openly.

'Sure am, Lady Kirk, Sir McAdams was his usual self! What have you got for me?'

'Ugh, that man! Did you know that a year ago he...' her voice trailed off as she realised the Sibyls had stopped their rummaging and were now listening intently. 'Uh well, yes you will be needing your full witches' sigil and a kit, just a few things on top of your basics. Let's get to the tattoo first and you can tell me all about it!'

Tessa grinned and gave her a thumbs up. Witch tattoos were not like the mundane version, instead of traditional ink a blend of willow bark and sage ash was used, much like the old primitive scarifications. This combination was sacred because it stored the magick chanted into it at the time of tattooing better. The witches' sigil was one of both power and protection, while also being a rather nifty form of ID as they sat dead in the centre of the chest. Lady Kirk did the best work around, and Tessa had always found it a pleasure to be tattooed by her.

The sigil was done in no time, and with very little pain thanks to the buzz of magick that came with it. The Sibyls had finally left with their pilfered goods, leaving Tessa and Lady Kirk alone to peruse the shelves of the restricted section.

'Seeing as they are throwing you straight into a case, we better get you set up with some nutmeg, musk and ylang-ylang for a truth charm... OH and you definitely need wormwood, dandelion and willow bark for a demon summoning, they are just far too useful. Probably some black iron, cascarilla and orris root for a bit of extra protection and some althea to boost your psychic skills to detect magick in a pinch. That will do for a start, but come and see me if you need anything specialised, OK?' Lady Kirk grinned as she threw each item into a sealed bag, as well as a few sneaky extras.

Tessa was about to thank her and leave but the Lady grabbed her hand tightly. Her eyes were bright with tears. Tessa had never seen Lady Kirk so pale and unhappy.

'Please, don't forget to summon your demon with a pure mind, after last week I, I...' Her voice cracked as the tears rolled down her rouged cheeks.

Demons, contrary to popular belief, were not inherently evil creatures. Their nature depended wholly on the person doing the summoning, so aside from being slightly sassy, a demon summoned for a good purpose would generally be good themselves. They were incredibly useful, being able to detect all forms of magick, walk on other planes of existence as well as being very good physical and magickal protection. All Agency witches used them regularly, and after their task was complete, they were sent back to Hel.

Unlike the popular fire, brimstone and torture concept of Christianised Hell, Hel was just the afterlife for the dead and home for the demons. Many books had covered the subject of Hel, although it was all rather stale. Utilising demons in this way was a good arrangement for all involved, as demons could not exist on this plane without a human anchor. Some demons considered it to almost be like a holiday.

Unfortunately, within the last week alone, a newly qualified witch had summoned a demon while angry about a personal problem and had unfortunately ended up in many tiny little pieces. Far worse for the other denizens of his apartment block, the Agency had gotten there too late to stop the wholesale slaughter of every person within reach. The surviving members of the Agency were all still shocked, but Tessa had to shake it off.

'I will be careful; I may not even need a demon this time. I might get lucky and have a really easy one, a pissed off faery or a magickal pick pocket!' Lady Kirk did not seem convinced at this, so Tessa just smiled confidently, packed up her kit and headed home.

Chapter Two

Her ancient Kingswood sedan coughed and spluttered into the parking lot, while Tessa attempted to soothe it with promises of an upcoming mechanic visit. Of course, this would have to be after her first official pay cheque had cleared.

When she had settled onto her sagging couch with a cold beer, she finally cracked the wax seal on her case file. She was confronted with images of a mutilated body, with sigils both burnt and cut into the flesh. Tessa fought the overwhelming urge to vomit, faint or just throw away the damned folder, but she forced herself to keep going. The body was barely even identifiable as male or female, the face and torso disfigured beyond recognition. Dirty tufts of hair stuck out here or there, but it was so clotted with blood the original colour could have been anything. Quickly turning over to the case notes, the wave of nausea hit again as she realised this poor mess of a man, apparently Mikal Myne, had been dumped in the gutter of an alley only a block away from her house.

Tessa resolved to make that little alley her first port of call, perhaps tomorrow, when the sun was well and truly up to wash away the spookiness. She flicked through the victim's history while taking another swig of her beer, ignoring her growling belly. Food was not a priority right now, and Tessa suspected that it would be hard to keep down in the face of these images.

With no recorded family, Mikal had been through the Agency testing systems and unfortunately had no skills other than necromancy, which had long been banned due to its lack of use for the greater good. Thus, he had been classified as a Restricted Innocent, and closely monitored to ensure he never used said skill.

According to the file, Mikal had been a good boy at least, and had a clear record as far as crime went in both the magickal and mundane worlds. It was unlikely that he had now done anything illegal enough to have warranted his death in the gutters of Bayton. Death may have been the norm here, but it seemed unlikely that it was related to any action on his part.

Necromancy was still taught about in Agency training and kept up in research, but it was deemed one of the Forbidden Crafts and practising the art could be punishable by death. This of course didn't stop everyone; it was mere months ago that the Agency had apprehended an unscrupulous factory owner who had put to work a literal force of zombies. The bodies had been secretly pilfered from a crematorium side business along with a few missing employees. Tessa had to admire the entrepreneurial skill of the owner.

Not that any of it helped him now. He was currently deceased and had his conscious and very sentient soul bound to his rotting body as punishment for about 20 years or so. Teaching him respect for the plight of the dead apparently. She had to hand it to the Agency; they certainly got creative with their sentencing. Death was not always the end when it came to magickal justice.

The death sentence was not handed down lightly. However, killing innocents was the best way to fast track such a sentence. Attacking an Agent was another way, although few were foolish enough to take that option.

The sigils didn't yield many hints. They were angular and aggressive, most done with a quick slash. Many were deep enough to show muscle and fascia beneath the skin. From what Tessa could recognise, a few were to increase power, a few were binding runes, nothing that really jumped out as a clear clue to intent of the crime. The only other thing of note in the photographs was that his right hand had been taken. Completely severed at the wrist joint.

Probably as some kind of trophy.

Tessa desperately hoped that this was some mundane murderer who liked to make their kills look like something magickal to waste everyone's time, but she would only know for sure once she went to the dump site. Seeing as she could only visit both there and Mikal's tiny apartment on the border of Bayton and Upton on the morrow, Tessa decided to give the sleuthing a break for now. The answers would be much safer to find in the sunlight, with other people round that weren't just out for shady reasons. Dark alleys were the least safe under the mantle of night.

Tessa grabbed another beer before unpacking her newest magickal supplies. She swigged away as she was making a few charms to sell. Little titbits for love, prosperity and confidence, all those small things people sought magick for. They were pretty, and Tessa actually enjoyed making them, despite the slight magickal drain. It was a nifty little supplemental money maker, using her Agency education to make various magickal items to sell at the night markets in the centre of Bayton.

The scrappy little market had set up in what had once been an industrial area, but it had long fallen into disuse after the economy slumped. The Bayton Central night market was a heady blend of magickal charm and ingredient sellers, food vendors, sex workers and the occasional poorly hidden drug deal. People of all kinds crushed in the dust together to buy the latest magickal fad or break a hex, while sating many more base needs. It was alive, and vibrant. The gathered people were peppered with buskers and performers, pickpockets and even the few urban fae, plying their own wares.

By the time Tessa arrived at her usual little stall she was almost salivating over the need to be part of this pulsing mass of humanity. It was so dirty and sleazy, while at the same time feeling more vivid than anything else in her life prior to now. The faces around her were in various stages of cleanliness, all with some kind of desperation etched into their lines. They came with what pittance they had made, looking for an outlet, a solution. Every now and then representatives from one of the old-world religions appeared to tout their particular mission, but most left rather rapidly. We were all lost causes for one reason or another.

The evening wore on slowly, and a few sales had come her way. Enough to tide her over until payday, or at least buy more beer. It was a necessity in her role, even if only to sleep. She was about to pack up her little stall when a familiar face elbowed their way through the crowd to her store.

'Ey Tessie! How's your lil bits sellin' girl?' At well over six foot, Damien Niel was a man mountain, tall and heavily muscled. He came oozing an aura of a man not to be fucked with, which helped greatly when you were the leader of the local gang. Damien oversaw the whole area in the centre of Bayton, although it was a power he used rather than abused. Overall, the citizens of Bayton Central loved the man. He had a reputation for fairness but tempered with ruthless protection of his borders and laws. It was a necessity in a self-governing area. The Agency, police and government all refused to touch the majority of Bayton.

Tessa smiled, genuinely happy to see his lean, mohawked face. Despite having extensive tattoos, piercings and a partially shaved head, Damien had thick glasses and a handsome smile. His Chinese origin gave him dead straight hair and eyes that crinkled into his wide smile. He invariably donned a pair of ripped jeans rolled up at the cuffs and a black shirt. Over the top he wore a long black motorcycle jacket that seemed to be reinforced with something heavy. It made the jacket almost appear like armour. Tessa surmised that it probably was something exactly like that, as Damien never went out into the streets without it, no matter the weather.

'Hi Dame... pretty good, 'nuff to get me dinner tonight and even have some change,' Tessa greeted him happily. She easily fell into the local accent, despite her upbringing. There was something infectious about the lexicon of the inner Bayton region. Being with Damien also made it worse as she wanted to fit in.

'Aw gal, whenna you gonna let me buy ye that dinner?' Damien said, leaning idly against the nearest surface while he carefully watched the crowd. How one man could look so relaxed, while at the same time being as menacing as a wild beast was always a mystery to Tessa. She didn't let his sweet words fool her for a moment.

'You only want to get me dinner to get me into bed, and I am not falling for that!' Tessa shot back as she packed up, making a mental note to stock up on love and lust charms. They always sold well before Valentine's Day, to sad people with desperation in their eyes... or pants. Topically, Damien looked pained, dramatically staggering whilst clutching his heart.

'Ye wound me Tessie, it ain't like that at all. Don't make me get one'a 'em love spells on ye girl, ye is cold assa grave.' Tessa rolled her eyes sarcastically for the third time that day. At this point it was a habit, one she was determined to break. She kept telling herself that the truth of her hesitation was that she valued Damien too much as a friend to go there. That and now she had images of severed hands and bloody sigils running through her mind. Which reminded her...

'Hey Dame, you know much 'bout that killing over on Straw Lane two nights back? Gotta case on it, 'n have to investigate it tomorrow.' Damien paused slightly while lighting his cigarette, the only sign that he was upset.

'Aye. Fella got himself carved like a Sunday dinner, then dumped there. Them Agency fools took long enough to get on it. It bein 'appening again 'n all.' He finished, taking a long drag of his cigarette. Tessa's heart caught in her chest, as her mouth dried. The world slowed as the realisation that this was not an isolated event flooded her body with adrenaline.

'Again? This isn't the first one?' she gasped, gratefully accepting a drag off Damien's offered cigarette to calm the storm of anxiety that had gathered in her stomach.

'Aye, your Agency ain't paid no attention when it one of our kind. 'E was all covered in 'em magick signs too, all carved up. But dem Agency don't care none. 'E ain't important enough. Bin two weeks now,' Damien seemed to be let down by that much to Tessa's surprise. For a gang leader he was pretty caring about those living in his territory. It was one of the many reasons Tessa gave him so much respect, along with the fact that he was effectively her landlord. He owned the entire market after all.

Still, she didn't like where this conversion was going, and now she had two deaths to investigate. So much for the 'domestic murder disguised as a ritual' idea. At the very least it looked like it could be a serial killer situation, the kind who liked to make their kills as weird as possible. While lost in her thoughts Tessa had fallen quiet, tapping her index finger on her lower lip. Damien cleared his throat quietly, to give her a little hint to move on and making her jump.

'Oh yeah uhhh well I'm gonna need to get all the details off you of this first killing, and... wait, where is the body for that matter?' Tessa almost shouted, realising what was missing. A few people nearby stopped to listen into the conversation.

'Eh buried. Dem bodies start a hell of a stink iff'n we keep em. Hassa bury em,' Damien said, implying that spur of the moment burials was entirely a normal occurrence in the area. Tessa couldn't help but be slightly disappointed, despite what a two-week-old body might smell like. She didn't suppose Damien kept a morgue handy, and the Agency didn't see fit to keep much in the way of facilities in this area. She sighed, the beginnings of a tension headache starting to throb its way into a vicious reality.

'Does anyone remember how the body looked? Was it dumped or...' she stopped as a smirk began to form on Damien's face. Tessa lifted an eyebrow.

'Done got better. Done took pictures, figure if that Agency don' do nuffin mebbe I do some'n, mebbe bring em to ye. But itta cost ye Tessie girl.' Damien's smirk grew into a self-satisfied smile as he finished, knowing he had Tessa on the hook.

'OK what'll it cost me? Better not get too greedy though, I'm pretty broke this month. Still on intern wages until next week.'

'Naw Tessie, ain't lookin' for money. Imma think I finally get that dinner with ye. Even pay and all. Like a real gentleman type.'

Tessa fought the urge to give a sarcastic response. Damien did not deserve it, but she just felt that it was all a little cheesy at this point. She was definitely not a romantic and did not enjoy the attention. That is what she tried to tell herself, anyway. Her reticence was a broken record by now.

'OK, OK. How about lunch though? I have to look at where the latest one was dumped, then look at his apartment, so after that?' she said, her traitorous stomach giving a growl.

'Aye, reckon I come with ye on the morrow, see 'em dump site. Mebbe them folks round there talk to you more if I'm helpin' ye yeah? Then I take ye to see 'em other dump site and have 'em pictures.' Tessa reluctantly agreed with a single nod, looking away to finish tidying up the last of her items. Damien moved over to help her, but every time their hands touched the little sparks of excitement skittered up her arms. Her stomach churned nervously, making Tessa feel as though she wanted to vomit. This was no help at all.

'Thanks for all your help, I uh, I better get home, be ready for tomorrow. You know, get my beauty sleep and all.' She said, ignoring the way he looked at her, the way her body responded. Rather than move out of the way, Damien stepped closer, into her little alcove.

'Damn Tessie, why can you never just let this happen?' he said, running a remarkably gentle finger down her face.

'Maybe... I... I...' Tessa's voice faltered, stuck between giving in to her attraction and her own resolve. Now was not the time to get attached to any man, despite how delectable this or any other may be. Damien smiled gently, realising that Tessa had revealed a tiny chink in her usual icy armour. Nervously she smiled back, just a little, ever so shyly. Any time Damien was in the vicinity her resilience was at its lowest.

Damien pulled her closer, cradling her face as he kissed her, and Tessa returned in kind. The dirty inner-city market faded, its junkies, grifters and pick pockets dropping out of existence. Her butterflies returned, warming their toes on the heat bursting from her heart. The moment of radiance didn't last however, and all the filth and sleaze returned in sharp focus as Tessa remembered her resolutions, and her employment. She slowly backed up, trying to think of something to say. Long moments of awkward silence passed until Tessa simply turned away and tried to lose herself in the crowd. She needed to eat, then get home and into her nice, safe, complication free bed.

It looked like she would have a busy day tomorrow including dealing with everything that had happened today, so she wanted an early night.

All the better to forget with.

She thought wryly as she fled, pushing through the crowds of people, her bag flinging out behind her.

Chapter Three

G rabbing a chewy pastry filled with mystery meat before she left and checking in with her few market friends had kept the severed hands and torn flesh from her mind for a while, but as soon as her head hit her pillow it came back. What did it all mean? The sigils had haunted her dreams, which made for a restless sleep. When her little retro alarm clock finally chimed, she felt as if she had risen from the dead. She dragged herself out of bed, cursing all and sundry.

Her cramped apartment was fiendishly bright in the mornings, and this one was no different. Tessa sat naked on the bed, caught up in her sleepy thoughts. She always knew that Damien had liked her for a long time. He had never made a secret of that. Slowly, before she was even aware of it, she had begun to have feelings back for him. It helped that Damien had always been a perfect gentleman to her and had never pressured her or made her feel threatened. What on Earth was she going to do about it all today? All she knew right now was that she had to haul her naked ass into gear. Tessa wandered slowly into the bathroom, yawning and scratching her frizzy mess of a morning hairstyle.

Half an hour later she was primped, preened and ready to go. She had it down pat, and a hell of a lot of concealer helped with the lack of sleep issue. A quick coffee, as dark and muddy as swamp water, and a short walk later Tessa was at the dump site, staring numbly at the wall. Dark magick clung to every crack and crevice, completely destroying her hope that this would be at all simple. She stared up at the muddy red bricks, towering up each side of the tenements around. Dirt alighted on each, greasy with unknown muck. Some parts had soft respite in the form of small patches of moss, the only plant to grow in these parts.

The dark magick may not be visible, but she could feel it, dripping gently from each brick like the dubious water that often flowed down the sides of inner-city buildings. She memorised its signature, its etheric scent. Powerful spells carried the unique mark of the caster, something that could be tracked and identified. This was sweet, disgustingly so, and woven into it was pure chaos. The caster was not sane in any sense of the word. That was a given really, as evidenced by the bodies of the people they had killed.

Damien appeared out of the shadows of what Tessa assumed was an intersecting alleyway, grinning at her in his usual idle manner. He was acting as if last night had never even happened. Fine by Tessa. She preferred to work without distractions.

'Hey witchy-poo. Find any good'n?' he growled in his casual Bayton soaked accent.

'Yeah, work. This place is saturated in bad energy and residual magick. Whatever was done here was... ugh I can't even fathom it right now. And I just can't think of why anyone would do this. Now that I know there is real magick involved there must be a reason, a ritual purpose... but I can't think what it is. All the sigils, it is all too vague, there has to be something here I'm missing... What devilry is this? Sorry, I was thinking aloud,' Tessa finished lamely; becoming aware she was tapping her lower lip absentmindedly again. She had also fallen into her classical literary language. Damien smiled slowly and lit a cigarette.

'Some sick people out'n Tessie girl, all kindsa crazy'll do anyfin fer any reason. Just gotta flick'm switch n dey go,' he muttered, idly scratching the regrowth from his now pompadour hairstyle. Tessa nodded, still frowning as she scoured the street and wall of the alley where the body had been, now only hinted at with a brown stain. Here and there seemed to be deposits of some sort of powder, but there was too little to make sure.

Still, she noted it down in her notebook, picking at the residue. At the same time, she noticed a slightly herbal smell from it, although she couldn't pick exactly what it was. She tried to scoop up as much as she could into a little bag with her small knife.

There were no visible sigils or the like on the wall or floor, but considering how many were on the body, that wasn't surprising. It wouldn't be necessary to do anything around the body. All of that power would come from the body alone. Damien cleared his throat loudly, much to Tessa's annoyance. As she turned to tell him off for interrupting her thought process, she realised they weren't alone. A scruffy, obviously high woman had oozed out of another alley to stand by Damien's side. She was short, tottering unsteadily on extremely high heels, with an ugly scrap of material on her lower half and a very revealing piece of lace on the top half. Tessa tried not to gag from her... pungent odour, as she walked over to them.

'Eh Tessie, this be Marie. She one who first seen the deadie. C'mon girl, ye tell'm what ye saw,' he said to the clearly shivering girl, a stern manner creeping into his normally relaxed demeanour. This was serious. She looked infinitely pained but spoke up.

'Aye, him dead good, gots no hand. I look him over and he all mauled up. Ain't seen no one round, but him all got powder on him, ain't drugs or naught. Smell like them magick stalls at the market, I done seen 'em. Done smelled 'em,' she finished, wavering on her heels as if the effort of simply talking had drained her. Tessa couldn't help but feel disappointed. A smell like a magickal stall could be anything, but she had the feeling the girl wouldn't remember the specific smell if she stuck it right under her nose. As if to prove a point, the girl took a massive snort of off-white powder from a small knife that seemed to come from nowhere. Damien nudged her shoulder when she was done.

'Ey girl, you finish up eh, give it to her.'

Tessa raised an eyebrow while Marie fished around in her bra, stashing her knife and finally producing a filthy purple baggie. The second the bag touched her hand, Tessa felt sick to her stomach. She was riding a wave of pain, and it swiftly drew her away from the physical world. It felt as though her own magickal power was being pulled from Tessa's very core. Quickly she dropped the baggie on the pavement, and abruptly the feeling of the evil leeching magick receded.

Digging through her patent red and completely impractical bowling bag, Tessa pulled out the tweezers she usually kept for an eyebrow emergency and her own knife again. Gingerly she pulled open the bag with her makeshift tools, keeping her bare flesh well away from it. The stench of blood magick flooded out of it, making her gag. This was the source of all the evil that clung to these walls, and they pulsed with power upon its return.

Damien and Marie watched her, one intently interested, one completely blank. Tessa used the tweezers to carefully pull out the contents. First came a small bundle of herbs, clearly starflower, echinacea and mugwort, followed by a piece of gauze with black, defiled blood, a black feather, a few hooks, one half of a lodestone with gold feeder dust all over it as well as a tiny scrap of copper with a rune she could not make out.

Times like this Tessa wished she carried her magnifying glass on her. And gloves for that matter. Blood magick made her even less keen to touch the damned thing, but she had to keep and research it.

'Well Tessie, what'n think all this litta bits is bout? Got'n reason?' Damien drawled, leaning back on the wall behind him. Marie had gone, probably slunk back into the alley to enjoy her high.

'Not really. I mean there is blood to bind it to the caster and as a sacrifice, a black feather for mystical knowledge. The herbs... I mean starflower is usually for courage, but it might be psychic skill boost, and it's mixed with mugwort, which is usually all about astral projection. It's all held with echinacea which is to make a spell strong. It doesn't really make any sense right now. Then there's a lodestone... it could be there for a good purpose, but the whole thing reeks with bad magick. I need to find out what this sigil is here, and have a think,' with that she stuffed all the parts back into the bag. Emptying out a collection of poppets, she used the plastic bag to keep the evil baggie in and added zip lock bags to her mental "Disgusting Crime Scene" shopping list.

'Aye, well'n that case Imma get us onto the other spot eh? See'n what's there,' Tessa only nodded in response, not worrying about the apartment now she had a second death.

Damien held out an arm, indicating the direction to go in and fell into step beside her as Tessa walked by. So distracted by her thoughts, Tessa allowed him to just escort her through the alleyways and streets until they came up to his gritty old muscle car. She jumped into Damien's car without really noticing, and it was only after they drove off that she realised this was the first time she had been in his car.

There was a pendulous silence brewing.

Tessa cringed at the awkwardness. She pulled out her folder of notes to cover her reaction.

'So... ummm... so where is this other dump site?' she asked, kicking herself for not asking before getting into the car of someone who was still a powerful gang leader. The man may be sweet, but there was still an inherent danger by association.

'S'over on the other side o' Bayton, down em South parts. Ain't so far... hey Tessie? Ah... ummm...'

'Wha?' mumbled Tessa, only half listening as she re-read her notes.

'Uh nothing,' Damien replied, realising that he didn't have her attention at all, before turning up Nekromantix' Horny in a Hearse to fill out the silence. Tessa tried to ignore the music that spoke of a ghoulish love.

He kept his word, and they arrived at yet another small dingy alley almost identical to the last before the next song ended. This side of Bayton was becoming rather small, a feral urban area surrounded by the scourge that was suburbia. Unfortunately, gentrification was encroaching on their little dystopia more and more every day.

The Impala Damien prized had ground to a halt almost on top of the old dump site, and while diminished, the residue of that same evil magick still filled the air. Tessa moved quickly, searching the walls and floor for anything of interest, but aside from the remnants of a recent drug trade, the alley was bare. She hadn't really expected much after all this time, but she still hoped. Damien had waited quietly by the car as she made her passes, the *shink* of his lighter flint being the only thing to break the relative silence.

'So where are those pictures? I guess it's better to look at them while I am actually here,' she finished hesitantly, quite frankly she was wishing she was anywhere but here. Damien nodded, pulling a creased envelope from his back pocket and handing it over silently.

Luckily for Tessa these photos weren't anywhere near as shocking as the first lot, and it was clear that the murderer was just warming up. The same sigils were present, again with some burnt and some cut. The cuts were shallower, hesitant and more jagged. Here was a bind rune, there was one to raise power, and another one she did not immediately recognise. She jotted them all down in her notebook, and sure enough, they were exactly the same as the other murder. She noticed also that the bodies had been arranged in the same way, legs and arms akimbo. It would almost be a normal spread-eagle if it wasn't for the uncanny similarities in positioning. The stance brought to mind the Vitruvian man from art history lessons at her reviled private high school.

Then she noticed something that made her gag in horror. All of the lacerations had been done before the man had died, with extensive blood collection in the skin around most of the cuts. Quickly Tessa ripped the Agency's folder out of her bag, but the pictures could almost be carbon copies as far as timeline. Both men had been tortured by having symbols carved into their flesh while still alive, and probably conscious. Tessa snapped the folder shut angrily while suppressing the urge to run home and hide from the serial killer boogie monster. All the Agency training in the world could not prevent the visceral reaction that these moments inspired. How had no one heard this torture? Surely, he had to have screamed the neighbourhood down. Or was it done elsewhere?

'I don't suppose you found one of those baggies on him, did you? Who found him?' she asked, tearing her eyes from the pictures.

'Eh t'was street kid, I fink Bomber was 'is name. Di'nt mention no baggie, but Imma question 'im on it real good when I see 'im,' replied Damien, growing angrier as he went. Tessa resisted the urge to shrink away, feeling intimidated by the man who was previously so familiar to her. Just when she thought she knew this man, he would reveal another facet, and her perception of him was forced to change. This was the gang leader.

'I better talk to him too, I guess. Who was it? The first decedent I mean,' she asked, trying to keep her voice from shaking. Damien scratched his head almost thoughtfully.

'T'was a fella called Scupper to us all, but reckon I'm the only one, know 'is real name. 'e was Adam Reeves.'

Tessa raised a well-drawn eyebrow.

'How is it that only you know his real name?' she asked, somewhat suspicious of his knowledge. While it was expected that the gang leader in the area would know a good deal of detail, and Damien cared more than most, this was unusual individual detail.

'E was my brother. Had a different Pa, but he was my brother all the same,' Damien fell silent, an emotion running across his face that was quickly stifled. 'So when 'im was found like 'is we thought mebbe it be a gang thing, but I still think it gotta be done, 'n find it all properly. So I took'm pictures, thought I'd ask round. But there ain't no bit goin'. Thought mebbe you help me bein an investigator 'n all,' he finished, blushing slightly before he turned away. Tessa tilted her head, confused about the blush, but she quickly dismissed any deeper meaning. Now she understood why he had been so oddly diligent when suspicious deaths were par for the course in Bayton.

'We will find out why these deaths are occurring Dame, and find who did them. I have no doubt they are connected. I might get us some help too, with all of that magick around they might be able to sense something more.' Tessa mused on the idea, this did seem like a good time to get a little demonic aid, and it was protocol to do so. Plus, she was slightly off put by a body being dumped so close to her home. Having a resident demon would be handy for her nerves.

'Don't want some other Agency goofball sniffing round me none,' he said mulishly. Tessa could practically see him digging his heels in. She sighed, finding it both frustrating and endearing. If it was one thing she understood, it was the value of privacy.

'It's not like that, I was thinking of summoning a demon to help, that's all. It's the protocol on a case like this.' She almost audibly groaned as Damien's eyes bugged out of his head. The Agency and other magickal users may know the truth of demons, but much of the hoi polloi did not, clinging desperately to the old ways. Something about the devil you know, and all that.

'Look, I don't really want to explain it all in this alley, it gives me the creeping willies, can we go get that lunch and I can tell you all about it,' she said, trying not to be frustrated with the ways of the mundane, especially this particular mundane. He was one of her favourites. Those were rare.

Chapter Four

D amien obliged with the promised lunch, whisking them off to a lovely hole in the wall diner, which had the most amazing burgers she had ever tasted. Tessa sighed happily, munching on the last few fries on her plate. She gazed around at the tacky décor, everything vinyl, red and glittery. The food even came in red plastic baskets. The silence grew, and Tessa focused intently on a dusty plastic plant to avoid acknowledging it. Damien however, could not contain his curiousity.

'So Tessie, you bin sayin' on 'em demons?' said Damien, leaning in conspiratorially. He had an excited look in his eye, as if he was about to be made privy to some secret societies' great knowledge. Tessa couldn't help but giggle at his secretive behaviour.

'Well there isn't much to it Dame, we summon demons, they help us with our investigations and then we send them back. The whole idea that demons are evil was part of the whole negative PR campaign against witches. Truth is, they are just an ordinary, natural being. Just like the fae, and guardian spirits. There is any number of other beings out there, and we are discovering more all the time,' Damien nodded thoughtfully, taking a sip from his soda. Tessa was impressed at how well he was taking this.

Mundanes were usually far more sensitive to such topics. Perhaps it wasn't so foreign to a man who witnessed the underworld of humanity. As an Agent Tessa had found that the worst monsters in the dark could be human. At least the so called evil beings were just living up to their nature. Although perhaps she was the one overthinking this conversation.

'So what do 'em all look like? Dey all red? Got em hooves and horns?' he said curiously, eyes bright at the idea of a stereotypical horror movie demon. Tessa laughed, almost spitting out her last fry. She had to take a sip of her drink before she could answer, choking on potato pieces.

'No, not at all. They look just like us, but have horns on their head. Demons may have once lived amongst us, becoming our gods. They are supposed to be immortal, and have great magickal skills. It would explain why almost every culture had a horned god of some kind,' Tessa stopped to finish her soda, lecturing about demons was thirsty work.

'So 'em demons, dey be just like'n you an' me? They could be anywhere around, but with they's horns covered? How come I never seen it before?' he asked suspiciously. Tessa thought on it a moment.

'Well I guess not too many Agents come into... that part of Bayton much,' said Tessa, trying to be as delicate as possible. People born into the slums of Bayton rarely left, and it was well known that the Agency avoided the area as best it could. Officially it was determined to be too much of a risk, but in reality, the people in the slums of Bayton had been thrown in the too hard basket. There wasn't enough funding for the effort required. Add in the general reticence of the lower socio-economic groups to work with anyone in law enforcement and it was a tempestuous blend.

'Yep, we don't like none law-folk nosing round. Ran 'em off a good long time ago. Cept'n ye Tessie. Ye is real special to us. I remember when ye first came to us, all fancy, ain't many tattoos or nuffin. Bin about 3 years now ain't it? Bin knowin' ye for a long time, bin loving ye for about as long. But I ain't sayin' it till now. Always thought ye might get bored with us folk, go back to yer fancy life. But ye stayed, ye stayed here with me,' Damien stared deep into her eyes, making Tessa cough and shift in her booth seat awkwardly.

It wasn't that she *didn't* want the hulking chunk of punk before her but dating the local slum overlord while working for the law was slightly conflicting, even if she only had jurisdiction over magickal crimes. The lines did not blur well.

In her awkwardness Tessa really noticed the noise of other diners, the scrape of metal utensils on ceramic, the smell of various greasy foods blending into a sickening cacophony. It was all too much.

'Thanks Dame, it has been a long time. Working at the market got me through my apprenticeship and paid a lot of my bills. I really owe you for trusting me, even being an Agent. I promise I will do everything I can to help with your brother, to make up for it,' she blurted out to make it all stop.

'Naw, Tessie, it ain't that, I...' Damien was cut off as Tessa checked her phone, jumping out of her seat when she realised what the time was.

'I am so sorry Dame, I gotta get all this back to the Agency.'

'Aye Tessie, ye go get it all worked out. Ye be knowin' where I am if ye need me,' Damien dutifully saw Tessa back to her car, waving curtly before loafing off to his own.

Tessa called through to the Agency archive sibyls to request all they had on file for Adam Reeves, to collect when she came in. It looked like Tessa would have a full afternoon of reading files and starting the preparations to procure herself some demonic help. This mess was ramping up and Tessa had a feeling she would need the help soon. Her first solo case was already threatening to overwhelm.

Chapter Five

There was very little in the file the Agency kept on one Adam Reeves, simply that he had been born in Bayton Central, gone to school in Bayton Central and had never gotten out. It didn't even say he was dead yet, which she could amend with the help of the pictures she now carried in her bag. The only other information was the results of his compulsory testing.

Interestingly enough, he had minor skills in clairvoyance and necromancy. It was the latter which rang alarm bells in Tessa's mind, and could be the link between the murders. She jotted it down in her notebook and returned the file. She needed to go see Lady Kirk before she left, to get a few more demon-ey items and ask her about the little baggie that still spewed vile will in her bag. As she walked the hallways of the Agency, Tessa could see people staring at her and weaving out of her path, clearly sensing the evil thing.

She was deep in thought as she traversed the stark white halls of the Agency, and barely had any warning as she was suddenly nose to nose with Mike Schimpf, co-hunter and royal pain in Tessa's ass. Typically of his type, he was short, fat and balding, with grease emanating from every haughty, arrogant pore. Oddly enough he had to be barely forty. Life had not been kind to the man; however he was equally an unkind man.

'Con-tessa... what a joy it is. I hear they allowed you to become a hunter. I'm sure there are plenty of occult dabbling housewives for you to bust.' Tessa tried not to shudder at the slime positively drenching every word from Schimpf's mouth. His nasal voice always seemed to creep over her, sinking into her flesh and making it itch fiercely.

'Sorry Schhhimpf, I can't tell you what I am working on. Toodle pip!' she could, but he didn't need to know that. In fact, the less he knew about anything to do with Tessa the better.

'Oh come now, Con-tessa, you wouldn't have gotten anything that important. Stop pretending to be a hunter and go back to serving tea,' Schimpf said, full of his own smug filth. Tessa simply shrugged, unwilling to play his game while she had more important and less smarmy things to do. A minute spent thinking about Schimpf was a minute wasted.

'As I said Schimpf-ey, toodle pip.' With that she flounced down the hall, trying not to break into a run to put some distance between them.

When she got to Lady Kirk's rooms, Tessa was still furious, but that didn't last long when she saw the latest collection of oak chests that had just come in. They were covered in inlaid brass magick blocking sigils, freshly cleansed in salt and moonlight. It would be perfect for storing that nasty little baggie, so she grabbed one along with a fresh metal dish to burn magickal herbs in, some extra candles, powdered sulphur, elecampane and mullein for the summoning. Some instinct told her she would need a rather strong demon for this case, and she trusted it.

Lady Kirk was rearranging the protection charms when Tessa found her. She grabbed an extra charm for herself while she was there.

'Tessa my dear, back so soon? How is your case?' she said, her milk and honey voice making it all better. Tessa smiled grimly, hesitant to share the dark reality of her case with the sunshine that was Lady Kirk.

'Well it's definitely not a pissed off faery!' she said wryly as she pulled out the baggie. Concern flashed across Lady Kirk's face, she could also feel its evil pull without even opening the drawstring.

'Where did you get this from? It feels vile!' Lady Kirk refused to take it from her hand, holding out a flat medical dish usually reserved for tattoo supplies. Tessa dumped the baggie on it as she replied.

'It was on one of my murder victims, which is a totally weird magickal situation without the baggie.' Lady Kirk raised an eyebrow but continued laying out the contents of the bag with some little tongs usually reserved for working with herbs. 'So, these were hidden on the guy, and when I held it, I felt I was being pulled out of myself, something was draining me, but not just energy or power, it was... everything,' her voice cracked as Tessa tried not to break into tears at the memory.

Clearly it had been more traumatic than she had originally realised. Having her magick, her power, torn from her felt invasive. Lady Kirk nodded, her usually jolly face now dark with concern as she handed Tessa a fistful of tissues. With a watery grin, the Agent jammed the tissues hard into her eye sockets, now feeling angry at her emotional response.

'No wonder. See these herbs? Echinacea provides power to a spell, this one is starflower which in this case would be for psychic skills. This last one is mugwort, and its normally for astral projection, but it can be used as an aid to break into a mind and keep it open. The little hooks are to ensnare someone and bind them in the spell, and the feather is for another mystical way into a person's mind in this case. Now where's my magnifying glass?' Lady Kirk dug through the drawers in her desk before she pulled out a massive and beautifully ornate magnifying glass that had to be an antique. She held up the scrap of copper, turning it this way and that to see its detail. She gasped loudly, pulling out a piece of paper to copy the sigil onto with a sharpie stolen from her tattoo station.

'That's it! Look for yourself, it's a sigil, a bindrune with Sowilo for power, Naudhiz for fulfilling a need or desire and Perthro for hidden or secret gains... oh my Tessa, this is a sigil designed to steal power, probably directed at a magickal skill given the other items. The blood there, well I guess it's the caster's, to direct where this power goes. I would bet there is a partner to this lodestone somewhere to help with that transfer. What have you gotten mixed up in my girl?'

With each of Lady Kirk's words Tessa's heart sank. She had expected this from her experience with this evil little bag, but having it confirmed was making it uncomfortably real. Even copied onto paper, the bindrune felt acrid and wrong. She recognised it in seconds.

'That's the same sigil used on the body too.' Tessa mumbled, fully dejected in her revelations.

'Used?' asked Lady Kirk, cringing at the thought. Tessa had hoped she wouldn't hear that.

'You don't want me to clarify that any further,' sighed Tessa. 'But what I don't understand, my Lady, is that they only really had skills in necromancy. And they weren't even particularly powerful. Why go to all this effort of making this powerful charm for people who had a skill that barely registered on the Agency's tests?' Lady Kirk grinned as if she were the child in the playground with a big secret.

'That's the thing Tessa, all this gold feeder dust would feed up that skill and amplify it. The bag is to get the skill, and you can then feed the stone as much as you want to boost it.'

Tessa sighed, unhappily seeing how much of the dust was there, let alone what Maria would have taken, mistaking it for something valuable. Gold coloured stuff in Bayton didn't last long, no matter whether it was real or not.

'Hence all the bloody sparkly dust.'

'Hence all the dust. Anything else?'

'No, only this weird herbal dust. I'm sure I can recognise it, but I just can't put my finger on it.' answered Tessa, remembering the other dust as an afterthought and pulled it from her bag. Lady Kirk raised an eyebrow as she took the little bag of herbal dust from Tessa. It was rare that she got so stumped on a case. Tessa prided herself on her uncanny abilities, and the respect they garnered. Lady Marique had often bragged about her prodigal intern to the other Agents at the booze fuelled Christmas parties.

'Goodness me girl, you should know this from your Agency initiation and binding. This must be knotweed, to bind the spell flawlessly. This is so well thought out, and almost impossible to break. I am sadly impressed; this person would make an excellent Agent and student.' Lady Kirk looked wistful as she spoke, always the caring type.

Too bad they are a murderer, and would have to die by Agency hands, Tessa kept those thoughts to herself. The outcome was pretty clear in this case. Whoever they were, their days would be numbered.

'What am I going to do with this thing? Aside from shoving it in an oak box and keeping it the hell away from me. And what if there is more of them? No wonder the poor bugger was carved up with...' Lady Kirk flinched, reminding Tessa that she spent very little time in the field. The Lady had a rather weak stomach for the inhumanities people could inflict on one another, and had happily opted to take over the storeroom when the chance arose. She left the fieldwork to those who had the knack for it, instead providing invaluable in-house support.

'Well, you have taken this past forensics right? They might be able to find some more magickal or mundane clues. This will be pretty exciting for them.'

Tessa cringed, unwilling to admit that she had completely forgotten about taking the baggie or photos to forensics for further analysis.

'Lady Kirk, I feel so out of my depth here, I thought I was ready for this, but I feel like I am making silly intern level mistakes,' Tessa blurted out, trying to get a grip on her anxiety. Lady Kirk shook her head firmly.

'Tessa dear, Lady Marique was here in tears for the first two weeks when she became an Agent. Even Sir Schimpf has hidden amongst the herbs having doubts. Almost every Agent has come here in the first few weeks to help allay their fears. You will be fine, I promise.'

Tessa gave a watery smile and nodded before falling into Lady Kirk's offered arms. She had always valued the friendship of the older woman, who had even tutored her when she was being rushed through her internship. Now she realised just how integral Lady Kirk was to the Agency as a general mentor.

'I will take it down now, thank you Lady Kirk. Thank you,' Tessa sniffled, refusing to let the tears truly take over.

'Time to get your demon, girl, chances are that the caster of this spell knows someone is after them, you did after all, touch this with a bare hand?' Tessa nodded miserably, realising the significance of her mistake.

'By the way you said it drew you in it sounds like it took a little of you too. When you get it back keep it in the bind box and keep safe.' Lady Kirk finished, dismissing Tessa gently as others entered the rooms. Tessa bowed and left, vowing to call herself up a little sulphur-based help as soon as she could.

She was still pondering her task ahead and her bizarre case when a familiar stench stopped her short of running into Schimpf again.

'Well well Con-tessa, can't even run your own case without help. I always knew you weren't cut out to be a hunter, but this is just pathetic, needing someone to hold your hand, especially *Lady* Kirk.' A sneer spread across his reddened, fat face as he spoke. He was acting as if he had won some kind of contest against Tessa by catching her consulting with Lady Kirk. She smirked back.

'Are you following me Schimpf-ey? Not got anything better to do than sniff after my tail like some kind of unsterilised street dog?'

His jaw dropped as she walked off, failing to find a comeback. She was elated to leave him gaping in the hall, blazing her trail to forensics.

Dropping the baggie off to forensics went well enough. They were appreciative that she had only touched the contents with her tweezers, however their joy of an untainted piece of evidence was quickly quelled when they were told it had been pilfered by someone completely foreign to the concept of aseptic technique. They promised to get as much information as they could despite the contamination, then return the bag to Tessa. She thanked them and headed out to finally go home.

Chapter Six

Back to my palace, Tessa sarcastically thought as she jiggled the key in the corroded lock on her front door. Finally getting it to turn, she rammed her side into the heavy wooden door, forcing it to pop open. The wood creaked loudly in protest of the abuse. Slamming the door closed again, Tessa dumped her bag on the couch and made a beeline for the kitchen and copious amounts of coffee. She would need it tonight, after a full day of work and needing to go to the night market.

There was no time for a nap, so Tessa jumped into the shower to refresh herself. The warm water welcomed her with steaming tendrils, promising to wash away her worries. For the briefest moment it did, and she could escape the issues around her feelings for Damien, murders practically on her doorstep and yet more severed hands.

The markets and an extra bit of cash called to her, so she quickly dried on a threadbare towel. Opting for comfort on this cool night, Tessa grabbed out leggings and a cherry printed dress. A quick brush and bump of her fringe and a protein bar later, she was ready for a night of serious wheeling and dealing.

Unpacking at the night market always took so much longer than she expected, and tonight was surprisingly busy. Plenty of people must have had a bone to pick, she sold out completely of hexes and hex breaking spells, as well as protection amulets. Ecstatic at the good sales, Tessa still couldn't help but be distracted by the absence of Damien tonight. He almost invariably made his rounds to check on each stall holder, as well as patrolling for any conflicts... or competition.

The sellers, sex workers and dealers all had to operate within his strict guidelines, and with that came his protection and security. All drugs needed to be quality, any dirty batches meant that dealer and supplier were out. All sex workers were regularly tested and had full health care if they chose, as well as a place to stay if needed. Damien had legitimately created an unlikely underworld utopia through sheer force of will and savvy business decisions. This meant that people came from miles around to partake in his venture, known for both its quality and quantity. It was why the market had flourished in the centre of his territory, and why so many people now resided here.

The time to pack up came quickly due to being so busy, so Tessa had to remain disappointed. Throwing all her items into her carry bag and jotting down her total sales in a notebook, Tessa felt like she was being watched and studied intently. Looking around furtively at the crowd of people around the market revealed nothing obvious. Still, she could feel a prickling at the base of her neck, like an invasive eye was roaming her. Quickly she threw the notebook into the bag, zipped it up and rushed off.

Choosing not to linger today, she made a break for the alley she parked her car down. The uncanny feeling went with her, making Tessa stop and check behind her to see that she wasn't being followed. Someone may have marked her for making a good amount of money at the market today, or perhaps the murderer had already made a move against her. The alley before and behind her seemed clear, so she simply quickened her pace, her heels clicking loudly and echoing aggressively though the narrow passage. Luckily, she had opted for heeled boots today, and she could run if needed.

Reminding herself that an Agent should never be scared, but be prepared, Tessa grabbed her keys out of her handbag. This way she would be ready to jump into her car as soon as she reached it. She could hear no other footsteps aside from her own echoing taps. Still the feeling urged her on, and she felt immense relief when she finally reached her car. It may be a decrepit rust bucket, but at the moment it felt like an impenetrable fortress. As soon as she was seated Tessa threw the car into gear and sped off.

Even when she was in the relative safety of her own apartment she felt ill at ease. Grabbing a beer, Tessa took long gulps to try and calm her nerves. She was in no frame of mind to raise a demon now. It would have to wait for tomorrow, as she rather valued keeping her neighbours alive. Tessa spent most of the evening on the couch, staring at the door as if someone would burst through at any moment, brandishing half a dozen zombies and some kind of weapon. Eventually she fell asleep there, falling into a fitful and nightmare laden sleep, the only sleep it seemed an Agent ever got.

Chapter Seven

The morning dawned bright and loud, but Tessa still managed to sleep in until lunch time. Endlessly thankful for her autonomous line of work, she stretched her cramped body out. Her neck ached with tension from sleeping the couch. Groaning with both the joint and muscle pain, sitting up felt like a chore.

Apparently, she had been more afraid than she realised, as her taser and knife were cuddled up on the makeshift bed with her. Checking her phone decided the course of the day for her, forensics had emailed to report that there was little extra information to be collected from the baggie. There was also a desperate missive to collect it immediately as it was creeping out all of the staff in the lab and interfering with their work. Tessa briefly wondered why they didn't just stick it in a bind box, but resolved to go get it as soon as she was ready. While blood magick was unsettling, clearly everyone else felt it was far creepier than she did. She quickly dressed, swilled a coffee and grabbed a protein bar for the road. The troubles of last night were soon forgotten in the central Bayton traffic.

The Agency building stood as tall and imposing as ever with its blank white facade. Plain and utilitarian. Utilitarian was really a word to describe the entire Agency entity as a whole. Agents weren't trained to be creative, but rather quick, decisive and clever. They were simple weapons of the Witch's Council; in the same way the mundane police were weapons of the government. Each Agent only had to think for themselves as far as solving a case and killing or imprisoning the criminal. The rest of their movements were up to the powers that be in the Agency and Council hierarchy.

It was no wonder that Tessa felt that she did not fit in with her co-workers. She had always felt like an outcast, caught somewhere between her role as an Agent, her friends in the Bayton slums and her past life as a young socialite. Not one of those factions were who she truly was, so she felt on the outer of all three.

Catching her previous mentor in the foyer, Tessa stopped to say hello to her former mentor Lady Marique. Towering above all Agents around her, Lady Marique stood well over six foot tall. She had once mentioned that in her tribe she was considered short. They had jokingly called her the runt. Tight lipped as to where her tribe was actually from, Tessa only knew it was deep in Africa somewhere. Lady Marique had been well known for her magical skills, so much so that the Agency had brought her over to Bayton, to help control an area known for its magickal crimes.

'Lady Bale, I have not seen you since you graduated to being a full Agent. How have you been? I heard they gave you one of the most challenging cases we had. You must have impressed them to get such a case,' she said, her eyes bright, however many more grey hairs had appeared since Tessa had last seen her. Her accent was soft, as was her gentle voice. It had always soothed Tessa in the most desperate moments. Lady Marique was a stickler for protocol, but she was also a damn good Agent, one of the best.

'Thank you, Lady Marique. I guess it is. It's not a particularly nice case, but I suppose there is no such thing as a nice case,' Tessa quipped, trying to seem light-hearted. Her eyes burned with fatigue, and Lady Marique was clearly not fooled by her facade.

'Dear, I trained you for three years, and you are still trying to pretend everything is fine? Now what is eating you?' Lady Marique asked, leading Tessa to a corner further from the foyer and the prying eyes and ears of the public. Tessa smiled weakly, of course her mentor had seen straight through her mask. Lady Marique had been more of a mother than her own birth giver.

'It's nothing I can't handle, just sleeping at night is a bit of a challenge when your victims end up mutilated right by your home." She rubbed her aching eyes wearily, not wanting to worry Lady Marique, who likely had a nasty case of her own to stress about, and probably a new wayward intern.

'Oh, I see. Yes, I am afraid you never get used to that. Now you are no longer my student I can say that on cases like these, wine and a bit of THC before bed really helps with that side of things,' the older Agent said with a wink. Tessa felt her jaw drop, seeing her strait-laced mentor in a new light. Lady Marique simply laughed and continued. 'I may be old, Contessa Bale, But I am not a dinosaur,' Lady Marique teased gently.

During her internship, Tessa had never heard her mentor speak in this way, and now she was no longer an intern she was privy to a whole new side of the Agency staff.

'I, yeah, I see your point. Although you are barely old,' Tessa retorted, to which Lady Marique chuckled loudly and bid Tessa farewell.

The forensic technician on duty practically threw the bag at Tessa as soon as she went through the door. She opted to barely touch it, having her oak wood box at the ready. Tessa slipped the forensics report into her case file and mentally prepared herself to take on the investigation of Mikal Myne's apartment. She had never really discovered where Adam Reeves lived, the Agency file only listed "no fixed address". She hadn't asked Damien about an address either. Given the type of people the murderer went after, Tessa figured it was highly likely that these were murders of opportunity.

Chapter Eight

Mikal lived in a sprawling set of notorious apartment blocks, all geared towards those with minimal income. They were the kind of estate where developers had tried to cram as many people into as small a place as possible. It was also clearly built as cheaply as the lowest tender offered and was now slowly imploding.

Mikal Myne had a pretty standard apartment, and the inspection yielded nothing of any particular interest. It was small, cramped and many of the "facilities" were not working. The man lived a plain existence, with beige and white making up most of his décor, takeaway containers choking up a full bin and a large television. Porn made up most of his watching selection, judging by his DVD collection. Even a search under the couch cushions only revealed stale snacks and crusty tissues.

Nothing really stood out, so she headed home, cracked open a beer and updated her case notes. There was nothing more that she could do for now, so Tessa began the process to summon a demon. First step was to clear her mind for the summoning, focusing only on very precise thoughts. She created a space in her living area, then opened all the windows to get some fresh air in.

Summoning generally ended up with a lot of sulphur around, and she wanted to clear that stench out as soon as she could. It was not a desirable smell, that of rotten eggs permeating the shoe box she called home. She set up her new fire dish, laying her herbs and a sterile boline next to it. Unfortunately, a summoned demon had to be bound to a living witch, which required living blood. Tessa wasn't squeamish, but cutting herself was never fun, and she really disliked the scars it caused on the heels of her hands.

Casting her salt circle, Tessa closed herself in with the fire dish to protect both sides of the thick, grainy line. She dumped carefully measured handfuls of herbs into the dish before lighting it.

The sulphur would go on last as it had a tendency to be a little volatile. Chanting quietly, she started fanning the dish until the smoke plumed forth. While she had never done this spell by herself before, she had studied the constituent parts individually and done it with her mentor many times. With a carefully measured movement, she dug the sharp blade into her hand and dragged it gently across the heel of her hand, just barely enough to release a few drops of blood. Tessa held her hand out, letting her blood fall freely into the waiting herb dish.

Finally, she felt the magick respond to her, rising in plumes around her as the smoke did. Continuing to chant under her breath, Tessa threw in the sulphur last as she said the final binding words of the incantation. Contrary to popular belief, magickal spells did not involve the magickal words shouted aloud. It would be annoying and highly impractical, especially when working in law enforcement. She would be very unpopular with her neighbours too.

'So mote it be!' The smoke billowed forth wildly, cut out most of the light in the room and the spell was complete. Tessa coughed a little as the smoke cleared quickly thanks to the open windows, revealing a hulking form in the middle of her living room. Tessa was careful to take a step forward, while she had been involved with many summonings before, she still got a little worried about her solo efforts.

'Um, hello?' she queried, the form starting to take on some actual shape. *Was that a pompadour?*

'Why hello there pretty little witch,' came the reply, in a rough masculine voice, something befitting size of man/immortal it came from. Tessa tried not to stare as a face Elvis would envy was revealed, dark eyes, long sideburns and a hint of stubble framing sensuous lips.

Just below an impressive pomp were curved black horns on either side of his forehead, the only hint of his true origins. The look came complete with rolled up jeans, black shirt and leather jacket, nothing like any demon Tessa had seen conjured before.

She had to resist the urge to gasp aloud or swoon dramatically, rather tempted to do both. Realising how awkward she was being, Tessa finally shut her gaping mouth and stammered a greeting.

'Oh, uh, hi. My name is Tessa and I will be your witch for today,' she said, hoping her attempt at wit would cover for her rampant staring. The demon nodded.

'Uh huh, and you can call me Lee.'

'Lee? I thought you would have a... well something more demon-ey, like Azrael or something.' Tessa asked, genuinely surprised. Lee snorted with laughter before shaking his head.

'First, that is a rather spicy angel. I do have such a name, but Lee just sounds better and I love me a bit of Jerry Lee,' he added, an infectious smile spreading across his face, making her stomach do little flip flops. This sure was an attractive being, now standing awkwardly in her lounge room, waiting for instruction.

'Well uh, you do know that he shot his bass player?'

'No, what? When? How?' Lee peppered her with questions, shocked to the core.

'Yeah it was like, the seventies. He also beat a bunch of his wives... allegedly." Tessa explained as Lee panicked. She figured it was time to change the subject. 'Can I ask you something?' asked Tessa curiously.

'Shoot,' the demon responded. Tessa was struck by how open his face was, and how kind his eyes were.

'Well, I don't imagine there are oodles of rockabilly demons just waiting to be summoned, so how did you manage to come out so perfect?' Tessa blurted out, blushing furiously at the last words. Lee laughed again, with a wicked twinkle in his eye.

'During the summoning, a demon is chosen that best suits the environment that we are going into. We are also given up to date clothes for the time and region. Even language is all sorted out. It is all very convenient and means that we can fit in to the society we land in. Aside from the horns of course. Apparently, they are a metaphysical necessity to ensure that we are never confused with humans. Perfect ay?' Lee gave her a few quiet seconds to get truly awkward over it all before continuing. 'You're not exactly the standard witch either, it's usually summon, debrief, and get to work. Unless of course, you called me here for another reason.'

A knowing look and the languid inflection in his voice indicted he probably wouldn't object to a summoning for more sensual desires. Tessa coughed nervously, those 'sensual desires' very much playing on her mind right now. She almost felt his caress as he looked at her.

How fickle am I? Tessa thought, reminding herself that Damien had been making her feel this way only days prior.

'Well, we have a case of at least two killings, and it seems like someone is taking their necromantic powers in the act,' Tessa said in a rush, getting all hot and bothered by the entire situation. He nodded abruptly before speaking.

'Ok, crime investigation, got it. That's all well and good, but you are bleeding all over the place, perhaps we should deal with that first before you give me all the details,' he ducked his head at her cut hand and the blood that was now slowly dripping onto the floor. Tessa visibly jumped, having forgotten all about the required wound on her hand. That managed to kill her frisky mood rather quickly.

'Oh right, I better get some...' she trailed off as she spotted the tissue box on her coffee table, grabbing a ball of tissues and stuffing them into her fist. She mopped up the drops of blood on the floor before throwing all of the tissues into the still smouldering fire dish. Even in her own house you couldn't be too careful with blood, if it fell into the hands of someone who held a grudge... well there was a lot of creative and sadistic ways you could use blood in magick.

'Heh, damn spells make a mess. So uh, I need to go man my market stall, do you mind if I leave you here with the case notes to catch up? You can eat or drink whatever you can find.' She said, waiting for his nod before showing him the kitchenette and other areas of her apartment. Lee seemed pretty content, poking around in the fridge then stretching out on her shabby couch with the case folder and TV remote.

She grabbed her bag and supplies before wishing her house demon a good night and jumping in her car, all the while wondering what the protocol was on demon housing arrangements. They weren't really taught that in the internship. Tessa supposed that sleeping on the couch had to be acceptable, and if not, well it wasn't her first scandal. It likely wouldn't be the last either.

Chapter Nine

The markets seemed strangely quiet tonight, with fewer patrons. Most opted to cluster around the food vendors with their dodgy little wagons. Nights like this she was glad that this stall was only a supplement to her income, she certainly couldn't live off this. As she was packing up she saw a familiar man mountain hulking toward her, scattering the last of the people between them. She smiled a rare genuine smile, as opposed to her polite sales smile, at the sight of him.

'Evenin' witchy-poo, 'ow goes it?' Damien asked as he leaned against his favourite pole, lighting up his usual hand rolled. Funny how this was becoming such a comfortable and familiar moment to Tessa. He flicked another of the nasty spell bags onto her table, clearly having spoken to Bomber. Tessa resisted the urge to ask about interviewing the kid herself, clearly it was not going to be an option. Damien must have had to put the fear into Bomber.

Instead, she quietly put the spell bag into another zip lock bag and answered him with a sigh.

'Hey Dame, not a good night, not many people here buying. Haven't hardly broken even.'

'Been noticin' that meself. Tryin' ta think on whassup down 'ere. Been asking round but ain't found anything on it,' he finished, taking a drag. Tessa waved her hand, dismissing it as a concern when there were much bigger and bloodier ones to think about.

'Down days happen. So, we think these people are being killed for their powers, which are being amplified as they go. Someone is collecting necromantic power.'

'You mean 'im raise'm dead?' Damien looked surprised at the thought. Tessa was pleasantly surprised he knew what it was.

'Well possibly, or use their knowledge, control the dead, and some are even rumoured to be able to just cause death with a thought, or a quick incantation. Plenty of bastardry to choose from when it comes to necromancy. That's why it is such a forbidden thing to study. It even roughly translates as death botherer in some languages.'

Tessa chewed her lip, thinking about all the consequences. It really painted a rather bleak picture, come to think of it. This nutter had to be stopped before any of that happened. Sudden movement in her peripheral vision caught her eye and she instinctively jumped, but it was only Damien moving closer again.

'You look so pretty when you think witchy-poo. Bein' so smart 'n so pretty, i's perfect. Gonna come to lunch with me again tomorrow?' he asked quietly, reaching out to touch Tessa's face, but she pushed his hand away reluctantly.

'I... I'm sorry, it just can't be like that. I am just really not looking for, or ready for anything. I can't get romantically involved with anyone because of my job right now,' she said, regretting having to do so more than she thought she would. A flash of hurt and disappointment flashed across Damien's face, but as always it was quickly quenched into his usual mask.

'S'all good Tessie, I getcha. You change ya mind 'n let me know, eh?' he nodded as he spoke, rubbing the back of his head. Tessa felt wrung out as she nodded back, mouth too dry to speak.

She had thought to ask Damien for some spare clothes for Lee, but it didn't seem like the kind of thing she could really ask now, given the conversation. She threw the rest of her bag together and bade a hasty retreat, skipping dinner in favour of getting out of there as soon as possible for the second night in a row.

As she walked down the usual alleys to get to her car Tessa was struck again by how few people were around that night.

Normally there would be a few lurkers, people peddling a trade in the shadows and so on. The idea gave her cold shivers down her spine, so she dug her knife out of her bag and palmed it. Just the feeling of its antler and bone handle calmed her, the runes decorating the blade glinting with the magickal sigils she had carved into it. Just its weight was bringing back memories of weapons training as an intern.

The training of an Agent was not just magickal but also physical. This included martial arts and weapons, all Agents were trained up to be physically dangerous. Unfortunately, this was not an ongoing regimen, and many of the seasoned Agents lapsed, such as Schimpf, and of course, Sir McAdams. Despite Tessa's general dislike of exercise, she had loved the various martial arts classes and had kept up with her training.

Spending time traversing the alleys of Bayton was also an excellent excuse for keeping her skills sharp. There were plenty of muggings and mundane crimes to go with the magickal crimes Tessa investigated. She did not want to be bested by some mundane petty thief in a back alley when she had taken down magickal masterminds with Lady Marique.

Tessa's car was within sight now, its rusty bonnet visible at the end of the alley. She fought the urge to run, instead quickening her pace until the tattoo of her modest heels echoed through the empty buildings surrounding her. There was always something innately creepy about dank, deserted alleyways, although Tessa tried to tell herself it was silly, not to mention rather odd for an Agency witch to be scared by the same alley two nights in a row. Reminding herself that this was the alley she traversed almost every day did little to soothe her. She was almost at the end when she heard the noise.

A shuffling, heavy breathing, with a slight moan that all those-who-had-once-lived-but-now-didn't kind of noise.

It didn't take an Elder to realise there was a zombie in the vicinity, especially given that there was some nutter interested in necromancy trawling through Bayton. Tessa held her knife in front of her as she tried to work out where exactly they were. Almost like props from a psychobilly band film clip, a pomped and tuxedo clad male shuffled into place behind her, while a beehived and pencil skirt-ed dame stepped between Tessa and her car.

Two against one didn't seem so bad when the two tended to shuffle, but they also didn't stop until they were in little pieces.

Tessa sighed, taking one last internal, wry giggle at the irony of actual zombie rockabillies before lunging at the female one, stabbing her in the shoulder and using her knife to lever the arm out of its socket. The female zombie clawed for her eyes with its other hand, but only caught Tessa on the shoulder, dragging long and dirty gouges into her flesh with her manicured but rotted nails. She took a moment to see where the male was, but luckily it was still making his way up the alley, hampered by what seemed to be a badly broken leg, amongst other injuries.

She turned back to the female, who seemed to be confused as to why she could no longer use her arm, Tessa danced in again, getting ready to pop the other arm. The zombie reacted to the movement and swatted Tessa away with an ease the undead really shouldn't have. Propelled through the air by the blow, she hit a trash can. While the aluminium can saved her from a direct run in with the wall, Tessa still dropped into the gutter like a cast off beer bottle. She groaned as she got on her hands and knees, needing to be up before the zombies could get the jump on her. They had now joined forces, trapping her in the grimiest portion of the alley. Slowly she backed up as they advanced, slashing at them when the opportunity presented itself, trying to cut tendons, muscles, anything.

By the time Tessa's back hit the wall of the alley the male had a limp arm and a slash across his throat, causing his head to bobble dangerously on his neck, while the female was missing her arm entirely. Overall, Tessa was not really better off, especially with a severed arm now being wielded as a club against her. The pungent limb hit the wall next to her head with a juicy splat, while Tessa struck out again with her knife, this time taking an arm off the male, and incidentally, his ear. The smell of rotten flesh and open intestines filled the air, more so when she was finally hit with the severed arm. It almost knocked her to the floor with its pass and left a bloody, congealed calling card across her face.

The zombies were close enough to lunge now, but in a stroke of luck for Tessa the female went first. The creature fell on her in a scratching, moaning heap. This was the moment she needed, and ignoring the painful pangs of exhaustion in her arms, Tessa brought the knife down on the neck of the female zombie. This served to sever the spinal cord and thus render it motionless. It wasn't deactivated but it also couldn't do anything aside from glare and snap its grimy teeth at her every now and then. The champing would almost be comical if it wasn't such a dangerous situation. Tessa rolled to the side to throw the incapacitated zombie as far as her aching arms could manage, working hard to draw in a dazed breath as she tried to scrabble to her feet.

The male zombie chose that moment to attack, jumping on her back before burying his rotting teeth into the meaty part of Tessa's shoulder. She knew that she didn't have to worry about catching the zombie-ness, it was more a raging case of septicaemia she had to fear. She cursed loudly, the pain making her vision go dark momentarily and they both fell forward onto the female.

It was a soft fall onto her rotting belly, the source of the open intestine stench, but that barely made it better. Tessa clawed weakly at his face while trying to blindly stab him with the knife that she had blessedly held onto, but she was losing a lot of blood, and consciousness. The world began to bleed into sepia tones.

Chapter Ten

An overwhelming stench of sulphur launched Tessa back into her body and less than a heartbeat later the zombie was dragged off her, taking a good chunk of her shoulder meat as he went. She cursed again, flipping over in time to see Lee snapping its neck and throwing it into the gutter like a rag doll. He walked over to help her up as casually as if he were taking a Sunday stroll, but the concern in his eyes revealed how he really felt.

'Why are you always bleeding when I see you, little witch?' he said, looking carefully at her shoulder.

'Well, I just wanted to look tough really,' Tessa responded, her wavering voice making her sound anything but. "Some new scars to really mix it up. Saves me getting a new tattoo."

"You must be OK if you're still being sarcastic. What was all this about?' Lee asked, handing her a wadded-up piece of material that looked suspiciously like a handkerchief. Tessa grimaced as she pressed it to her wound, pulling the chiffon scarf out of her hair to make a makeshift bandage.

'I assume it's about the case. The asshole knows who I am by my magick. Wait how did you know I was in trouble... scratch that, how did you find me?' she asked abruptly, her brain catching up to the situation as her head started to clear from the initial adrenaline haze. Unfortunately, that clarity came with an intense increase of her pain. It was blinding.

'Your blood runs through my veins, it's part of the summoning process. I know where you are at all times. I will find you whenever you need me.' A rush of heat skittered through Tessa at his words and she felt a blush growing. She was at a loss for words, but thankfully Lee chose that moment to actually help her up.

The second she was upright her legs buckled, making her fall into Lee's waiting arms. The blood loss must have been worse than she had thought, and he had clearly anticipated her collapse. Tessa soon realised her entire left side was bloody, and the sanguine mess was mostly her own. He scooped her up gently, despite her protests, and carried her to the car. Tessa found herself being put into the passenger seat and her keys being abruptly confiscated. Lee jumped in the other side, gunned the engine and took off in a spray of asphalt and city detritus.

'How do you know how to drive?' she asked curiously, the pain in her shoulder now a dull throb as she floated between conscious states. The dirty lights of Bayton flew by with a dreamy haze haloing each. Streetlights and neon, soon lost in specks of rain beading the windows.

'Pfft it's not that hard, despite what humans seem to think. I can even produce a licence if needed.' Tessa blinked slowly, realising how well equipped he had come from the other world. Demons sure were handy. It was truly an effortless transition into the human world. Her world. One he could never be a part of. *Wait, why would she think such a thing?* Tessa caught the weirdness in her thought, but it was lost to pain.

Due to Lee's speeding and Tessa's semi lucid state, the journey to what was now their shared apartment seemed to take no time at all. Before she knew it Lee was settling her onto the couch and disappeared into first the kitchen and then the bathroom. He returned with gauze and armfuls of herbs including thyme, white willow bark and celery seed by what Tessa could see and smell. He had to cut off her shirt to get to the bite, but Tessa was in no state to be modest. When he pulled away the makeshift bandage it revealed a bloody, jagged hole in her pale flesh, filled with clots and sluggishly, stubbornly flowing blood.

He set the herbs in a bowl of warm water, gently reconstituting them while he washed the wound, getting all the zombie... bits out.

Apparently, a rotting mouth leaves rather a lot of flesh from the biter behind, as they both found out, with the help of Tessa's tweezers. After the horrors of the last few days, she would never use them cosmetically again.

Lee gathered the herbs into a wet mass and pressed it gently onto the wound, causing Tessa's vision to go dark again as the more astringent herbs burnt their way in. She started to keel over with a stifled moan of agony, but Lee held her up with one arm while using the other to bind it all with a fresh gauze bandage. Soon the willow bark and celery seed began to take effect, and Tessa could finally think again. While she had thought she would need to go to the hospital, Lee's expertise was helping her avoid that visit.

Truthfully, a visit to the hospital in Bayton Central may be more dangerous than the zombie bite. Public healthcare was about as effective as the law enforcement in her area. Hospitals were woefully underfunded, overpopulated and even being an Agent didn't warrant any kind of special treatment.

'I'm guessing whoever is behind the murders knows who and where I am, maybe they got close enough to feel my magick at the market or something. I heard them, the zombies, coming, but there was nowhere I could go,' she said, a few stray tears escaping her eyes, much to her annoyance. It was bad enough she had been bested by only two slow moving zombies, now she was crying over it?

No way.

Tessa had always been known as a hard woman, on the outside anyway. The aggressive bullies at her elitist private high school saw to that. She hated to show vulnerability of any kind, especially in front of this attractive man. Demon. Man demon. Ohh lawdy, she was in a state.

'Hey, it's OK, you did well, I just helped out a little. I was getting bored of sitting on the couch anyway!' said Lee, giving her a gentle rub on her non-injured shoulder. 'After what I saw today, I think Hel-cat is a more appropriate moniker for you than little witch,' Lee quipped and was rewarded with a watery smile.

'I guess it's safe to say the little baggies are working, and they can raise the dead. I can't imagine there is two zombie raising psychopaths running around Bayton. Well, I hope not,' Tessa mused, shuddering at the thought. Lee looked quizzical.

'Well do you know how to stop the magick, or the zombies, without chopping them up? I am guessing they won't stop with just two,' he asked as he started to pack away the herbs and throw all the bloody wadding and clothes into a burn pile. Tessa stopped to think. Zombie busting wasn't really a subject she had ever covered in great detail. She winced as she levered herself up from the couch and slowly limped over to the bookcase, much to Lee's chagrin.

She dismissed the lecture he was about to give her with a wave of her good hand, grabbing her favourite tome on magick before settling back on the couch as just as the dizziness was setting in again. Lee marched into the kitchenette while she started to flick through the pages, skim reading all things undead.

He returned a few minutes later with a cup of tea, holding it out to her with a grin. Tessa wrinkled her nose at it, giving Lee a questioning look. She had smelled better odours in a well-used horse stable.

'The only other thing you have to drink here is beer, and alcohol will make you bleed more. The tea is sweetened and has olive leaf amongst other things, so it will stop you feeling so seedy. Just drink it girl!' He said, exasperated as she pulled a range of faces. Finally, she took a sip, quickly deciding it was a good idea as the throbbing in her shoulder and head gently subsided.

'How did you learn all of this?' she asked, wondering about both the tea and the poultice on her shoulder, which she could barely feel now. His herbal tricks had worked fast, certainly faster than it would have taken to go buy pharmaceuticals.

'Eh you pick up some *cunning* skills in four hundred years. Geddit? The poultice was taught to me by an old witch, almost two hundred and eighty years ago now. I'm glad you had most of the herbs used in the old ways, most have discarded them now. Medical advancements are great, but I do love the feel of herbs.' Tessa watched as his mind clearly wandered back to those days, stunned at Lee's rather advanced age.

To be honest, Tessa mostly had the herbs for their magickal uses and knew little of their medicinal uses. Modern times had a habit of ignoring such things. Perhaps it was to the detriment of the world, given the way Tessa was now feeling. A euphoric buzz had started to coddle her brain from the pain and the trauma of the day.

'Four hundred years? You have been around that long?' she blurted out before she could stop herself. Tessa lived in a world where age was a taboo to never be spoken about. Certainly, her mother had never acquiesced to ageing, and always lied when asked. Luckily, he just laughed it off.

'Yep, four hundred years of being at the beck and call of witches. It gets tedious. Plus, all the travelling. Being dragged to and from Hel is... odd.' Lee gave a quirked little smile.

'What's it normally like when you get summoned? I mean where do you sleep and the like?' Tessa asked, still unsure of what she should really be doing with this hunky demon in the down time. She reached for her notebook, jotting a few things down on zombies. The books she had on hand were yet to yield any great revelations.

'As I said before, it's usually all business, sometimes there's a spare room, sometimes the couch and quite often it's just the floor. Many witches seem to think the demons are just slaves, so they treat them like it. They remain wilfully ignorant to the fact that demons are still living, sentient beings. There have been demons who have been kept captive, beaten, and... more,' he finished, a touch of anger tainting his voice.

Tessa looked surprised and was about to say how she felt sorry for Lee when he stopped her by holding up his hand.

'It's OK really, people are getting much better lately. The times changed. I have heard from other demons how much better it is. Even if we must sleep on the floor still at times, we are treated better overall. Plus, I think I have it pretty cushy this time! Now what have you come across about zombies?' he said, definitively changing the subject, so Tessa let it drop.

'Well, while they no longer have a soul due to being dead, the magick used to create and control a zombie makes up for it. So, in theory you could actually banish it in the way you would a spirit or ghost. If a banishing works, it would actually be quite a quick and easy process. As far as I can see all you would need is some sloe, ajenjible, iron dust.... hmmm and possibly some graveyard dirt. I don't even think the dirt needs to be corpse specific. It could be as simple as just throwing it at them,' Tessa said, chewing the end of her pen as she thought, occasionally scribbling down some more notes as she estimated quantities.

'Yeah that all makes solid magickal sense. Do you have all of those?" Lee asked, staring dubiously at her empty kitchenette again. Tessa laughed and nodded, gesturing to her stash in the closet. "I suppose we might as well make some up tonight, I have a feeling today's attack was just a test. They are probably going to be back even as soon as tomorrow,' Lee said, while Tessa nodded again in agreement, still immersed in her studies.

Under her careful direction they spent the rest of the night mixing up different herbal blends. Her herbal induced buzzed feeling morphed into one of true contentedness.

Laughs were aplenty, and Lee was a font of knowledge. Tessa was impressed by his indomitable personality. She was truly enjoying herself for the first time in a fair while.

Unfortunately, unless Tessa wanted to dabble in necromancy, there was no way to test their new anti-zombie weapons. They just had to wait until their mysterious murderer tried again, and hope for the best. It wasn't the most comfortable position, but Tessa did feel a little more empowered having some kind of defence at hand.

'Be careful, Hel Cat. We don't know how well these would work in a tight situation. Please take me with you if you are going somewhere alone, OK?' Lee said, looking down at her as he passed across the last bag of herbs. Tessa gazed up at him intently, searching his face for hidden meaning in the caring words. The previous demons she had worked with had all been tasked with protecting their witch, however they certainly had never seemed to care about them on a personal level. In fact, they had barely interacted outside the job at all. As to the personal summonings, Tessa only knew they existed and had never investigated the finer details, despite her experimental nature throughout her Agency internship.

'Careful demon, it almost seems like you care,' Tessa retorted dryly, trying to cover her confusion the only way she knew how, with sarcasm.

'Aye little witch... just a little,' Lee responded, leaning in and bringing a hand up to cup Tessa's face. Her face flushed with a combination of shyness and passion, although she pulled away from the attempted kiss, muttering about needing sleep and retreating to her bedroom. She tried not to slam the door in her haste, lest Lee take her reaction as anger.

Chapter Eleven

The sun glared in at Tessa, rousing her from a deep sleep. She was made acutely aware that there was a pounding pain in both her head and shoulder. Groaning, she dragged herself out of bed and tiptoed around Lee, who was fast asleep half naked on the couch. Tessa silently crept into the kitchen to put the kettle on.

Dumping willow bark, skullcap and feverfew into a teapot, she yawned and drummed her fingers on the table, before it occurred to her to check her phone. With all the excitement of removing festering zombie pieces from her flesh, Tessa had forgotten that such things existed. Given the events of last night, she wasn't surprised that she had slept in till 11:30am, but the 5 missed calls was unusual. All were from Damien, and she was about to check her message bank when someone started rapping frantically on her door, keeping time with the pounding in her head.

Tessa cursed loudly as they continued to hammer at the termite weakened wood until she called out, her voice a strained croak. Lee had thrown himself into action and was warily standing to the blind side of the door. She nodded to him conspiratorially before cracking the door open just enough to see out, ready to glare them down. Damien poked a worried face through the gap, making Tessa jump back in surprise. The door hit the length of safety chain and rebounded into Damien's flushed face.

'You're a'ight, ye 'live, aye, bin scared all this'n talk about ye, n heard bad went down on ye 'n all.' He said, the words coming out in a tumble in his haste, making his rough accent worse than ever.

'Wait, slow down, what?' asked Tessa, thoroughly confused about what this garbled mess was trying to communicate. She unlatched the door chain and let him in. Before Tessa could fathom what was happening, Damien had scooped up her hands into his sweaty mitts, almost crushing them with his sheer size.

'Tessie, I just got done talkin' in town, 'n sommen' toll' me there been a girl got dead las' night. Then I hears ye done been attacked an' there blood all over wherein ye park ye car n I thought... wait who is THAT?' Damien stopped suddenly, catching sight of Lee. The demon had come out of his protective hiding spot and was looking decidedly partially naked in the middle of Tessa's living room. It did not look good in any situation, let alone this exact one.

'Uhhh Dame, meet Lee. He is...' Tessa began to say before being stopped short by an explosive outburst by Damien, accompanied by spit and sweat. His face was now a pulsating mess of veins, his usually carefully coiffed hair now flopping into fury burnt eyes.

'Oh, I see what'n all 'bout. Ye gimme the stiff las' night, ya all not ready n all an' I get all worried over ye, thinkin' ye dead. I thinkin' on I love ye and givin' ye time, but ye jus' wanna be playin' house with this asshole. Ye kin keep on with this creep.' With that, Damien glared at the both of them, turned on his heel and stalked angrily away. Tessa went to follow, but he was too fast, stride too long, and was gone by the time she even reached the main door of her apartment block.

Tessa cursed and returned to the apartment, both sad that Damien felt so hurt and peeved that he hadn't just let her explain. He hadn't trusted her, and that bit Tessa to the core.

There was no time to sit and worry about it however, from Damien's garbled words it sounded like there had been another death. Tessa pulled on some cute rolled up jeans and a bowling shirt before grabbing her bag and keys. Ready, she nodded to Lee. He had somehow manifested some new clothes and was waiting wordlessly by the door for her. The usefulness of demons was endless. This time he had donned a black collared shirt and blue jeans. Sensible, sleek clothes for inspecting a fresh corpse. Together they rushed out, and desperately begged the cantankerous old car to start. They both cheered as it turned over with a grumble and a screech. It was time to cruise through the filthy back alleys of Bayton, looking for a murder.

Even without Damien's help the murder scene was not hard to find. Despite being in blood soaked Bayton, every murder still drew a curious crowd. Especially bizarre ritual murders. They loved those, and news quickly spread. This time it was on the very edge of Bayton East, in what was actually a rather nice, calmly suburban area. There were little bits of green poking out here and there rather than the usual brown and grey monotony of the squalor in Bayton central. This was indicative of small gardens, public space care and money.

None the less there were still alleyways, and more to the point, murders to happen down them. Tessa had to elbow her way through the gathered people to see clearly. What was revealed had her immediately wishing she didn't.

The pools of blood were congealed and still, manifesting gory halos around the body, testament to the intense trauma that had occurred. Again, many of the injuries were done before death, but there were many post-mortem cuts that seemed to be more like mutilation than crafted sigils of any worth. Random slashes and stabs dotted the body, which did not occur in the previous murders. These cuts were deep, hacked and feral. The burns were through to muscle and bone, an impressive feat to accomplish.

This murder felt different. What had previously been precise care and attention to detail was now clear frustration. It was too messy. Oddly enough, this time the body had been merely dumped in the street, strewn aside like so much trash. There was no posing, and the right hand was merely hacked up rather than being cleanly removed. Tessa chewed her lip, pondering the lack of care. She threw out feelers for magick, and swiftly got her answer.

'Lee! It's because she died! That's why she was just thrown away like this,' she said, flapping her hands wildly in the excitement of her morbid revelation. Lee however, stared back blankly. He had been quietly standing by, subtly preventing the crowd from impeding Tessa's process.

'Uh, not to rain on your parade, but didn't they all die?' he said, one thick eyebrow crooked in confusion.

'No, she died too soon...' Tessa became acutely aware of her intently interested audience and lowered her voice, 'they must need the victims to stay alive to complete the spell and get their skills, that's why she is all mauled up but not with sigils. They got pissed off and just dumped her here. It's why there is so much blood here and so little magick. I can't trace it because it's just not *there*. The spell wasn't finishe... OW HOLY HEL.' Tessa stopped gesturing wildly towards the victim when her shoulder made an odd popping sound and began to hurt fiercely. The bandages on the wound rapidly filled with blood, staining her shirt. Lee resisted the urge to smack himself in the face over her silliness. This little witch was certainly passionate. To a fault.

'You do recall you got bitten, yes? Slip your mind a little? It will keep popping open until we can get some iron water onto it.' Tessa looked at him dubiously, wondering what on earth Mars water had to do with it.

'Yer whut?' she asked. Lee looked dumbfounded, shocked that she did not know this simple old remedy. He sighed before beginning his explanation.

'When a zombie bites it transfers a kind of hex that aims to kill you by bleeding out. Iron breaks most hexes and curses. Therefore, short of sticking an iron rod in your wound, you need to use iron water. Did they not teach you this before? This Agency of yours? The Witches Council? Anyone?' he asked while she looked at him quizzically. It seemed a total oversight to him that she had not been taught the simplest treatments for magickal mishaps. She did not even seem to understand the connection between iron and hexes.

'Uh it's not like you expect too many zombies running around downtown Bayton. It was only the basics, and even then, it was more about the necromancer. Well, how to track and kill them really. We certainly didn't cover zombie bites any more than the concept of don't get bitten. That and if you do get bitten, you won't turn into a zombie. Raising them as hitmen? No. I mean who even does that?' scowled Tessa, pressing yet another scarf to the wound and wishing she had packed some tissues at least. Lee sighed dramatically, wondering what exactly they were teaching the witches at the Agency academy now. He was slightly humoured by the clear brattiness of this formerly rich witch.

'Yes poppet, in the big wide world outside of this shit hole there is plenty of ghoulies and ghosties for everyone. Each with a different Achilles heel and a myriad of different ways to kill you. Better get born kid,' he said, ruffling her hair and making Tessa scowl even more ferociously.

'Isn't this what you demons are supposed to be for? The big protector and magickal consultant? Why bother summoning you otherwise?' she whined. Lee smirked at her words. Her freckles and upturned nose made this little temper tantrum even more endearing.

'Isn't this your job, baby witch?'

'Well, I suppose I will be all up on it when I am as OLD as you are,' she snapped, disliking how easily he could get a rise out of her. Of course, she couldn't help but feel snippy on a day where everything seemed to be going wrong.

'Ooh ouch, doll's got the devil in her today,' he said, glancing over as the crowd began to watch them more intently again, rather than gawking at the body. Whether it was a brutal murder or lover's tiff, it was all cheap entertainment in Bayton. They loved anything that broke the monotony of concrete and a daily struggle to live.

'They also didn't tell me how much of a pain in the ass demons were,' Tessa grumbled, turning back to the body before Lee could make some kind of comeback. She stalked around the mess of a human being some more in a huff, trying to pretend she was focusing on her work.

Finally, she was forced to concede that there was no more information to be derived from this poor, pathetic remnant of life. Her biggest hope of finding a victim with the magickal link intact was dashed with this woman's death. A quick survey of the gathered crowd revealed that no one had borne witness to the crime, and while the victim had been 'seen around,' no one really knew who she was.

After notifying those who would dispose of the body and inform the Agency, Tessa finally admitted defeat and headed to lunch as soon as the scene was signed over to the crime scene crew. They ate silently and voraciously, both starving from the missed breakfast, despite having just investigated the mutilated body. There was no way an investigator would survive if they could be put off their food by a dead body. The job was both disgusting and strenuous, so a good meal could rarely be missed. They learnt that pretty early in the academy.

'So, we know she died too soon, so there has to be at least one more body. Unfortunately, we live in one of the most populated areas for this part of the country. There is no way to determine who could be attacked next, nor somehow protect an entire city of people.' Tessa pondered aloud to Lee while still chewing her burger. She had hoped to have some kind of revelation, however it was Lee's face that lit up instead.

'Well, we know one thing, the necromancy is the key. We know the killer is using the powers, we know at least two of the victims had the skills. Is there some way we can scry for necromancers?' he asked.

'Forget scrying, the Agency keeps files on all the teenagers who are tested and have some kind of magickal skill. We can just search the database for anyone in Bayton who has those skills.' Tessa crowed with joy at the idea of narrowing down their search.

Pulling out her phone, she quickly called through to the Agency to request the search be done for anyone registered for necromantic powers. After she cut off the call, she high fived Lee in the dorkiest celebration. He couldn't help but smile at her antics. But the moment could not last, and as soon as lunch was done, they had to get on with their day.

Chapter Twelve

Tessa dropped Lee at home before heading over to the Agency to pick up the much-needed iron water to treat her bite. It had already popped twice since, once while giving an exuberant gesture to an ignorant fellow driver and once while slinging her heavy bag around. She dropped in to Lady Kirk's rooms, but luckily the Lady was caught up in a magickal tattoo so Tessa could grab her supplies and go. She didn't want to concern the older woman with tales of wounds and murders.

She wasn't so lucky with Sir McAdams, who required a full run down on the events leading up to and following her bite. Skipping over the rather steamy side of her demon, she gave him as full a brief as she could, including her theories on the girl dying and the subsequent loss of temper by the killer. The Sir simply listened, nodding quietly and handing her fresh bandages as she required them.

'So, what shall be your next move Lady Bale?' he asked, almost managing to be caring rather than sleazy for once in his life. She had felt the relief of the hex breaking almost immediately, Lee had certainly been right about the use of iron. Something snapped as soon as she poured it on, like a chain snapping from too much pressure. Flesh had already started knitting back together before she had finished pouring the water on.

'Search, Sir. I have authorised a search on anyone with necromantic skills flagged on the Agency testing. Then I have to begin with the people again. Surely someone saw something. There are three bodies now, without a magickal trail it's a matter of searching. I will head to the market and see what I can find. Sir, what should I do if I encounter more... zombies? I mean they are kind of people...' Tessa trailed off, lost in her own personal ethical dilemma.

'Kill them, erm- re-kill them. We shall return the bodies to the family, but the reanimated dead have no place amongst the living. You have your knife I take it, keep it close and use it. Taser is apparently useless. Bullets and lasers are only useful at a distance, so be prepared with a backup,' Sir McAdams said, with more sincerity and grim nature than Tessa thought possible. There was a darkness that seemed to cloud him as he talked. Something haunted his eyes, an echo of trauma in his words.

Tessa pondered the meaning of his mood as she nodded and excused herself.

As a hunter and Agency witch she was trained to kill, but something about taking out the bodies of unwilling puppets made Tessa baulk. Too bad it looked like she would be tasked with doing it with great regularity until this case was over. Who knows how many the killer could or would raise? Necromancers were largely an unknown quantity when it came to magick. At least she wasn't the one who had to return the bodies to the family and explain why they came back in pieces... Or why they had left for that matter.

As she was preparing to leave, Tessa's phone trilled, receiving the email about her search query. Thank goodness the archive Sibyls were so organised. Their system was impeccable, making it worth their generally ornery nature. Unfortunately for Tessa, there was over 22,000 people in Bayton alone who had tested positive for the power of necromancy and were still alive. This didn't even include anyone in the surrounding areas. There was no way she could even notify all the people of the risk, let alone protecting them all. Still, she dutifully saved the list, just in case. For now, it was time to pack up and head to the market to grab some much-needed extra cash.

Being back in the familiar sleaze of Bayton Central Market calmed Tessa, the heady air of smoke and food reminding her she was still alive.

She couldn't see anyone she knew in the scrappy crowds, so she headed over to her regular spot to begin setting up, only to find it already occupied. A dirty, feral eyed hag was filling her stall with pieces of dried animals and various odd powders in large plastic bags. Her stained hands left filth on every piece of stock, dandruff and dust raining down on her display. Oddly, Tessa could not smell the woman, something she was rather thankful for.

'Hey, what's this? This is my usual spot!' she said, trying not to let the anger in her voice show. The wobble in her tone betrayed her completely.

'S ain't no more. Dame done gave me this, ain't yours no more,' the women replied, a smug smile spreading across her grimy face to reveal blackened teeth and festering gums. Tessa fought the urge to shudder, sickened by the decrepit woman before her.

'But... this is my stall. It always has been. I need this.' Tessa was starkly aware that she was begging to the wrong person, and becoming distinctly whiny while she was at it.

'Eh, Imma needin' it more. Imma bin real good to Dame, an' he gimme this. 'S mine now.' Tessa huffed to express her displeasure, turning on her heel before storming to the rooms Damien kept overlooking the market. Her thoughts were mutinous, however she was complaining to the wrong person.

How dare he give away her spot to some pipsqueak who probably didn't even know what most of the things she was selling were used for. Dyed water and pickle powder. She was just some used up hag who couldn't keep her teeth in her head.

She banged angrily on the iron door, waiting for whichever lug was on door duty today to answer. Once admitted she stormed down the hall, not waiting for the usual escort and threw the door open to Damien's office. He jumped in surprise, automatically pulling a Colt .45 from the ether.

'How DARE you pass on my stall to some little bitch with a bagful of lolly water potions! What is the meaning of this?' shouted Tessa, panting slightly from the exertion of her angry tantrum and needing to steady herself on the door frame. It somewhat diminished her threatening bluff.

'What ye thinkin' ye is, comin' in here like that. Ye ain't got the right eh? 'S my market and I gonna put who I want in it eh?' Damien drawled in a monotone, but there was anger flickering under the surface of his words. The gun disappeared, but he remained on guard.

'But that was my spot! I have been selling there since I started!' Tessa replied, slightly aware she was beginning to whine again.

'Ain't no one's spot but mine. Ye got a replacement me, now I got a replacement seller. But I'm done lookin' after ye, *witch*. Ain't my problem now.' He stood up, motioning to the door guard and heading to his rather extensive private bar. The heavy stepped forward, filling the doorway and very effectively shutting Tessa out.

'Wait, Dame, what about the murders?' Tessa was forced to jump on the spot to try and see over the man mountain who was now trying to herd her down the hallway. She was rapidly losing ground.

'Like I carin' bout dem. Ain't my business now. Go ask ye fancy boyfriend.' Damien spat the final words before downing whatever amber liquid he had just poured. Tessa felt her heart jerk, remembering how angry he had been over finding them together.

'It's not like that, Dame, he is here to help, that's...' Tessa tried to explain, but Mr Tall-and-Meaty finally succeeded in prying her off the doorway and scooting her down the hall as Damien slammed the door. She was rather unceremoniously dumped out onto the street, spewing a litany of curses at all around.

Angrily pulling her cardigan around her, Tessa collected the few things she had left at the market and began to leave, trying to hold her head high. She had just stopped at the stall specialising in ritualistic animal bones when someone started shouting her name. Heading toward her was a slovenly woman, dragging an even dirtier and rather sulky long haired teenager.

'Hi Nari, what did you want?' asked Tessa, trying not to let her annoyance show at the interruption.

'Eh Tessie, you bin lookin' at them ones they got killed yeah?' Nari huffed, finally reaching Tessa and giving her another blackened smile. Tessa nodded in response, too exhausted to speak.

"S here be Skitch. He one o' my boys. Reckon he seen somethin' for you he did.' Now Tessa's interest was piqued, and she raised an eyebrow toward the kid.

'That true?' she asked Skitch, who seemed to be trying to shy away from them as best he could. He nodded nervously, his eyes darting around the crowd, jumping from face to face.

'Yeah, I seen 'em,' he said, finally settling on staring sullenly at the ground.

'Saw who? Skitch?' Tessa prompted when he didn't speak up.

'Seen em what dumped de girls body. She was real pretty,' he finished, scuffing at the dirt under his feet.

'Yes, I am sure she was, when she was alive,' she said, trying to keep him focused, a task that seemed akin to herding cats.

'Naw, them that dumped her was it. Was a woman. Real pretty woman,' Skitch replied, blushing furiously at his words and kicking the ground harder, deeply under the effect of gangly teenager hormones. Tessa felt floored at this little revelation, her mind ticking over like a demented hamster spinning on its wheel furiously, with no clue as to where it was going.

'So the person who dumped the body was a woman? Is that what you mean?' Tessa tried not to shout in his face, the kid was clearly scared enough already. He simply nodded, shying even further away from her. Nari slapped his shoulder, making him wince.

'Ye be talkin' boy. Ye be helpin' the Agency cop,' snapped Nari, glaring at the boy. The subtle threat was not missed by Tessa.

'Can you tell me anything about what she looked like? Anything you remember about her?' she asked more gently this time, lowering her voice and trying to play mama. The real mother just grinned on, flashing those rotten teeth that were the trademark of the area. The boy started to shake his head, then paused. He received a sharp jab in his back from his mother to get his mouth moving.

'Yeah she, she got red hair, but all pretty like, and she walk funny, like her leg don' work right. An she have 'em around her, people what are lookin' dead. But they movin' you know?' The words spewed forth as the boy shivered on the spot more from fear than cold.

'Yeah, I know,' said Tessa, her shoulder instantly aching in sympathy. The memory of being bitten by rotting teeth, the putrid gum flesh sinking into hers, was still fresh. 'Do you remember any details about her face? Clothing?' Skitch clearly thought hard about the response, but ultimately looked confused.

'Eh she be wearin'... a dress or somefin'. With... colours. An' she got red hair. Yeah, thats what I seen. That's... all I seen.' The last words were said as his eyes darted around the crowd again, as if he expected the red headed woman to burst forth and flay him at any second. Tessa knew she would be unable to get much more out of such a reluctant witness without dragging him down to the Agency interview rooms. They all stood together for a few awkward moments, unsure of how to finish up, before the mother broke the silence.

'Well, my boy been done talkin' an' we all hungry. Guess we gotta eat 'n all that. When he said he seen somethin' I tell him he gotta tell that Agency lady. An' he tell ye. He tell ye all he tol' me. But it be late. An' we all real hungry, but ain't we got no money eh... yeah, we all real hungry,' she trailed off, the twisted grin spreading across her face more and more as her eyes scanned the people around the market. Tessa sighed and fished around in her pocket for a $50 note and handed it to the woman before walking away, leaving a trail of blessings and desperation. She glanced over at her old stall one last time, to see the dishevelled woman grinning manically, taking great delight in her defeated retreat.

Chapter Thirteen

'You left me here all day. I was bored. Human TV sucks.' Tessa had barely gotten into the door before the griping started.

'Gee I thought I had conjured up a demon, not a lap dog with separation anxiety,' she snapped, still feeling raw from her market problems. It wasn't a massive loss of income, but it was a loss none the less. Lee looked mulish, but Tessa cut him off as he opened his mouth to argue. 'There has been a development. I spoke to a kid at the market and apparently the person dumping the bodies is a woman. A rather attractive red head by the sound of it.'

'Seems to be a few of those around here...' replied Lee, his pout now replaced by a cheeky smile. Tessa opened and closed her mouth a few times, unsure of what to say. Was the demon *flirting* with her? Now? His grin widened, and suddenly Tessa itched to kick him right out the door she had just entered. Oh, how she loathed cocky men, and she seriously hoped that he wasn't like that.

'Now look here, *demon*, if you're going to stay here you better cut that out and have some respect damn it!' she said, stalking up to him until they were eye to eye. Well would be if she didn't have to tip her face up so far to look at his eyes.

'It isn't all bad, is it? Some people even think it's charming,' he said with an exaggerated affectation to his voice and a flourish of his hand. Luckily his tongue was firmly planted in cheek. Tessa tried hard not to laugh at his shenanigans.

'You misogynistic ass! How dare you think you are so, oh!' she was cut off from her feigned sarcasm as he pulled her close to him, wrapping his arms around her and finding her lips with his. All of Tessa's stress of the day disappeared as they connected, a fizz of excitement running from her lips to her very toes. This is definitely the kind of distraction she had wanted from the day.

Still, she pulled back, the guilt over Damien still crushing her heart. Lee began to apologise for his actions, and they talked over each other in awkwardness.

'Wait! I can't...' she protested without any real wish to stop, but Tessa soon pulled him in again and found herself kissing him back. All those sly looks and fleeting lustful thoughts came to the fore, and she tightened her grip on his neck and pulled his body closer. Even after so few days, Tessa had already felt a need to intertwine with this man.

Their unspoken desire finally broke its fetters, and before she knew it Tessa was tearing at Lee's clothes. He hoisted her up into his arms as she wrapped her legs around him.

Blindly Lee sought out the ratty couch. As he walked Lee pulled off her dress, exposing the flesh he had craved ever since this unusual witch had called him forth. His pants were also waylaid, falling in a crumpled heap, revealing his long muscular legs and his preference for going commando.

Tessa sighed happily, feeling his fully aroused length pressed against her thin and holey underwear, warm and hard. She didn't have the mental clarity to worry about the fact that she had chosen an old and torn up pair of underwear that day, not that Lee even glanced at them. They both fell onto the couch in an ungainly heap, awkwardly sexy. They kissed long and hard while Lee fumbled to get Tessa's flimsy underwear off, finally doing away with finesse and simply tearing through the tattered lace. Tessa giggled at his actions, finding this sensual but animalistic side very attractive.

No wonder all those witches summoned demons for a good time.

Clearly mortal men had a lot to learn from their demonic counterparts.

Lee moved his kisses down to her neck, nuzzling into it as his hands searched out and found her vulva, slick and warm. She let herself sink into the pleasure like a hot bath, soaking herself in the hedonism of the moment. Lee delighted in the sounds of her contented moans, so engrossed in the sight before him that he missed her hand sneakily working its way in between them. When she took him in her warm little hand, he had to fight the urge to buck uncontrollably, to be in her, feeling the slick and warmth so promised. The urge to truly merge into her. It had been a long time since he had felt so close to someone, and despite the slight fear it caused in the back of his mind, he was well down the rabbit hole. With this little witch, he was terrified that it was more than just sex.

Finally, he ceased his teasing, pulling Tessa close and taking one last deep breath before giving into his urges and burying himself deep within her.

Chapter Fourteen

Tessa woke and yawned languorously, memories of her night flitting through her mind and making her smile. They had ultimately ended up in the bedroom, becoming well acquainted with each other's bodies until the early hours of the morning. Lee was still asleep, his long body sprawled across her bed, dwarfing it despite being on a queen-sized mattress. Tessa padded out to her kitchen where there was tea and her phone, dead as a door nail. She cursed herself for getting distracted and leaving it off the charger, but then grinned again at the thoughts of that particular distraction. Plugging her phone in, Tessa boiled the kettle and chewed her nails while she waited for it to charge enough to turn on.

The revelations made by Skitch still tossed about in her mind, the fact that they were now hunting a murderess and had a vague description was both heartening and worrying. They were still no closer to knowing why she was taking these lives, but Tessa was sure she would again. Whatever was happening, the murderess needed at least one more successful victim after the premature death of the last one. Her phone beeped and vibrated as it turned on, then again and again, almost scooting itself off the bench.

She sighed, the buzz of the previous night completely killed by waking to a full message bank for the second day in a row. Clearly something had happened overnight, and it required immediate attention. Sighing again, Tessa flicked off the kettle and threw on some toast, resolving to get ready and see what all the fuss was about. Coffee would have to be to go.

Within 20 minutes both Tessa and Lee were dressed and ready, her make up perfect, his hair coiffed to the gods. Tessa checked her phone whilst slinging on her bag, heavy with makeshift zombie weapons. The phone messages had all been from Sir McAdams, notifying her that a fresh male body had been found in Bayton East, a few alleys away from the previous murder. Tessa mused a moment on this fact.

Could there be some kind of cardinal points thing going on, perhaps to raise power and appeal to the elements?

She jotted a note down in her notebook then tucked her phone into its little pocket and headed to the door. Lee followed silently, still yawning from the exertions of the night before.

The second Tessa put her hand on the doorknob, she knew something was wrong. Angry power jerked up her arm like a swarm of bees, each one stinging viciously as they went. The room started to spin, but still she couldn't let the handle go. Her hand felt as though it was trapped in a vice, locking it in place around the doorknob. Her mind was paralysed, internally she was shrieking from the pain, but externally she merely trembled violently. Soon her mouth started to foam with bright red blood.

'Shit!' shouted Lee, before grabbing onto her and tackling her away from the door, none too gently. It felt to Tessa as if the flesh had been torn from her hand, such was the connection the curse had. They collapsed in a heap on the floor and Tessa finally managed to begin shrieking repeatedly with pain, pulling herself into the foetal position in Lee's arms. He held her close, rocking her gently until the screaming broke into whimpers and Tessa uncurled enough that he could check her out. All of her organs palpated well enough, and she hadn't continued to bleed, so he went back to simply comforting her. Slowly the haze caused by the pain lifted, and Tessa began to become coherent again.

'What in the Hel?' she said tentatively, looking herself over. Her hand had blistered aggressively, with forked red lines like veins running up her arm. It reminded her of a lightning strike victim. The rest of her felt back to a shaken normal now, but Tessa took advantage of a few more moments cuddled up in Lee's arms, seeking comfort from the shock.

'Well Tessie girl, I am guessing that you have been the victim of a rather nasty curse right there. You are bleeding again,' he said, pulling out a patterned handkerchief to gently dab away the blood spattered across her face. Oddly enough she actually smiled, then even laughed. Lee raised an irate eyebrow but continued to dab away at the mess.

'Sorry, I really appreciate the effort you are going to, it's just... who even uses hankies anymore?' said Tessa, breaking off into peals of laughter. Lee looked shocked and even a little insulted.

'Well... they're just handy damn it... and if you're complaining then you can feel free to clean up your own mess! This is the second time you have needed them; I might add,' he growled back, but he continued to wipe her face and hands gently.

Tessa decided to stop complaining, having an attractive demon concerned about her wasn't such a bad thing. The implications of it may be, but she pushed those thoughts out of her mind. Finally, he seemed satisfied and helped her to her feet.

'Salt?' he asked, heading to the kitchen when she pointed.

Tessa ran her hand over the door without touching it, feeling the pulse of evil on the other side. Lee returned with a huge handful of salt. He whispered an arcane word into it before throwing it at the door. The evil power bucked wildly, and a strong scent of sulphur filled the apartment. It took a few seconds before both dissipated fully. Still, when he opened the door Lee used the handkerchief to grasp the handle. When he finally swung it fully open, Tessa gagged at the sight.

At about chest height was a severed tongue, an iron nail impaling it and fastening it to the door. Below it was an occult glyph, viciously written in what appeared to be blood. Lee 's face reddened, clenching his fists before turning to Tessa.

'That was designed to kill you. Those bastards! I'll...' Lee stopped himself short of exploding in anger, knowing that Tessa was already shaken up enough. She felt a little relieved and safer that he held back.

'We will just have to stop them soon before they try again, OK?' she rallied, hoping to placate him. He nodded slightly, still flexing his fists. Tessa was right of course, but it didn't make him feel better right now. There was a part of him that was ready to tear apart whoever had just threatened the little witch he... but a demon could not consider such thoughts.

'I am teaching you how to put up wards on your door and windows too. I can't believe the Agency didn't teach you those either. They have gotten complacent lately and I will not have them put you at risk!' Lee looked down at her, an odd light in his eyes she wasn't used to. Tessa coughed nervously and held out her hand to be helped up as a distraction.

She grabbed her camera out of her bag and snapped a few pictures of her door before she wrenched the now defunct curse tongue and nail out of her door and put it in a baggie. It still felt vile, but as it was perishable evidence she had no choice but to put it in her little fridge until she could get to the Agency in the afternoon. She resolved to severely disinfect that fridge later... or maybe just throw it on a fire.

The streets were relatively empty in Bayton central, which wasn't really a surprise for a Saturday morning, as most people were still sleeping off the excesses of the night before. Bayton East was a little more alive, especially around the alley where the latest body was dumped, once again the usual gawkers filled the entrance. They now recognised Tessa, parting to allow her through, probably so they could get the fresh goss.

Whispers rippled through the crowd, every now and then a word like incompetent or useless was audible. Tessa kept her head held high and waded through, Lee following closely behind.

The body was splayed out in the same style as the others, the same collection of sigils present, their face turned away, so only long and bloody hair was apparent. Tessa turned back to crowd and scanned their faces.

'Does anyone know who this is? Anyone recognise him?' she asked, watching heads shake and feet shuffle. Somewhere up the back a reedy voice piped up.

'Naw we ain't moved 'im. He all covered up on 'im face.' A voice from the front responded hesitantly. The air was heavy with expectation, people drew closer to see if she would reveal the face. Tessa sighed.

So much for the easy way.

She began to snap the usual photos, carefully stepping around the body to capture every detail she could. Trying to only view the severed right hand through the camera screen, Tessa hoped to reduce some of the horror. Finally, Tessa could put it off no longer and leant in to pull the hair away from the face with a pen she would never use again.

Skitch. Her heart dropped as bile rose.

That poor kid who didn't even want to talk to her had most likely been killed for it. On a hunch Tessa levered open his mouth with the pen and sure enough, the tongue was missing. Ripped out. The street code for talking against someone's will. Not only had he been killed as part of whatever this was, it was also in an effort to not only attack her psyche but also to attack her with a curse. Tessa shivered violently, trying not to throw up. She knew it had to be his tongue and blood on her door.

'What have you found Tess?' asked Lee, the concern visible all over his face. He had felt the change in her demeanour, the fear pumping her heart into overdrive.

'Remember how I said some street kid told me it was a woman dumping bodies? Yeah, this is him.' Tessa fought the urge to cry as she told Lee. Whether it was rational or not, she felt responsible for his death. Lee simply drew closer and waited for her to finish, something she was immensely thankful for. She was so close to breaking down into uncontrollable tears.

Tessa felt that she should have done more to protect him, should have tried to get the Agency to protect him. A $50 bill was not worth a life like this, even if most Agency witches would consider him just some street kid from the sewer of Bayton. Tessa snapped a photo of his open mouth and then pushed away from the body, gulping at the air to stop from crying. She dug out her phone to call the poor buggers who had to take a body away for the second day in a row and sent someone to find Nari.

'So, ain't no residual magick eh?' queried Lee, trying to distract her. Tessa was about to ask how he knew before remembering who he was. Horns aside, it was rather easy to forget.

She felt the air around her, sending tendrils of her magick out. Nothing, aside from the remnants of the angry, defiling magick left in Skitch's body. Any ties to the caster or trails had well and truly gone.

'Nope. They seem to be able to time it perfectly. We can't track them at all.' Her shoulders hunched as Tessa realised once again, they were at a literal dead end. A 'pretty red-haired woman' did not give them much to go on, especially given how well the disguising glamours worked now, and how many pretty redheads were running around in the world.

Plus, the only person who had actually seen this pretty red head now lay dead with his tongue in Tessa's fridge.

The crowd began to disperse as the body van pulled up. Tessa spoke briefly to the Agency men who would take the body and run the autopsy, asking them to notify her if they found one of the baggies. Technically that was her job, but she couldn't bring herself to search him, not now. The last stragglers of the gathered crowd grew excited as they set the remains on a stretcher and placed him in the van, the morbid thrill of a local's final journey. Tessa looked them over, disgusted at the heartlessness of some people, before recognising a familiar face.

The wretched older woman who had taken her market stall grinned and waved at her from the front row, baring her awful teeth. Tessa resisted the urge to flip the bird at her, instead turning away to search the surrounding walls and floor beneath the body. There was little of interest, the same sigils newly marked over the old ever-present graffiti. The ground knotweed clung to the grime on the wall, scenting the air slightly. She took the appropriate photos and moved to the mouth of the alley, waiting for Nari to show.

After about 20 minutes of stress-chewing her nails and idly chatting to Lee Nari finally appeared, her face flushed a cherry red from having to exert herself to get to the alley. Looking like she was dragged from bed, Nari wore a singlet shirt with a breast peeking out one side and a pair of men's boxer shorts. Tessa pushed away from the wall she had been leaning against and walked out to meet her.

'Nari, on behalf of the Agency, we are so sorry for your loss. Did he tell anyone else about what he saw?' She asked in her best calming voice, although Nari only shook her head, while seeming distracted. 'I guess the person who did this must have seen him talking to me,' said Tessa, sadly shaking her head. Nari looked around her to where the magickal forensic and clean-up crew were working away.

'That where 'e was eh?' she inquired, the redness fading and her voice almost sounding disinterested. Tessa was rather surprised at her reaction. She had expected wails of grief, not this apparent boredom. Giving Nari the benefit of the doubt, Tessa tried to explain as gently as she could.

'Uh yeah, he was down there.'

'What it look'n like?' Asked Nari, with a definite note of curiousity in her voice.

'Woah, ummm well it was not pretty... not something a mother should see. Do you know if Skitch had any magickal skills?' Tessa tried to remind her that this was her son she was talking about in such a detached manner. Nari finally looked away from the crews and back to Tessa.

'Naw, not anyfin' we can make a dime off. Did em tests and it only sommat to do with em dead folks. But 'e ain't even really use 'em yeah?' she answered, now back to sounding utterly bored until some new thought crossed her wicked little mind and she practically beamed.

'Well, the way I reckon it, 'e was killed when your Agency didn't come through none, 'e was killed on your watch. Reckon that deserves me some com-pen-sation you know? Your Agency can gimme some of that financial compensation for all my 'eartbreak and all that. Cos I done 'elped em,' she said, a grin working its way across her face. Tessa's brain stalled at this reaction, she couldn't conceal how appalling she thought this woman was. Again, she had to resist the urge to slap someone senseless.

'You would do best to remember that was your son there, who only this morning was mutilated, tortured and killed!' Tessa hissed, pointing down the alleyway.

'Eh, got more of those. Can always make new sons. But now I don't got me a bigger one for getting us an income you know?' Nari shrugged as she spoke, each word making Tessa angrier and angrier. She pushed the older woman out of the way in disgust and summoned Lee to walk out too with a jerk of her head.

Let Nari rot for all she cared. While she had thought she knew what the general attitude was like in Bayton, she realised now that she had never fully understood how cold and vicious the streets were. Poverty made monsters of us all.

Chapter Fifteen

They drove home to pick up the tongue then over to the Agency in silence. Not even the car radio eased the mood, so she turned it off with an angry flick of her hand. Upon arriving she went straight to Sir McAdams' office, to report the events of the last few days, including her slight curse problem.

McAdams agreed that she must learn to ward her home, as well as organising a patrol crew to regularly check on her apartment for the duration of the case. Tessa was shocked by the severity of response but was happy to agree with it if it meant no more crucified tongues in her life. She had given her morbid find to the Sir, who quickly glanced at it before requesting that an intern take it to the forensic department. He flat refused to touch it. The poor kid paled when he saw what he was expected to carry, and Tessa wondered if he would ever be back to complete his internship after seeing that particular component of the job.

'Well Contessa, it appears you are doing well on this case, despite the setbacks. I am sure I don't need to remind you of the importance of a quick resolution, given the recent news,' Sir McAdams said, leaning back on his chair. Tessa racked her brains trying to think of a particular news story. Had they already been attacking the Agency after a murder victim had spoken to an Agency employee? Surely the media weren't that attentive, although Nari may have talked for an extra bit of income. Sir McAdams clearly noticed the confused look on her face.

'The uhhh attack which occurred earlier today on some teenagers who stumbled upon a group of shambling corpses hiding out in an alley? I did leave you a voice mail about it. Those kids used up three bottles of iron water between them. A clean up team already went in, but the dead were gone by that point. Here is the report,' he finished, handing her a thin envelope. Thoroughly embarrassed at missing this detail, Tessa thanked Sir McAdams and quickly left. She could review the report later, but for now she just wanted to hide her burning face and move on with the investigation.

More teenagers had been attacked on her watch. More... kids. It didn't matter that these ones didn't die. She was responsible for it. She was the shitty Agent, the great imposter. What did almighty magickal powers matter when she was unable to use them? When she was too incompetent to protect the street kids around her? All those whispers in the crowds, they were all right. Those whispers deafened her now, pounding through her head, as her heart beat faster and faster. The sound of it rushed through her ears. Her own blood, bombarding her eardrums. It was beating out a rapid tattoo of her failure. Tessa started to run in her panic. Her vision went hazy. Her breath came hard and fast.

Failure...

Imposter...

Incompetent...

Pathetic...

Useless...

Worthless...

Failure. Imposter. Incompetent. Pathetic. Useless. Worthless. Failure. Imposter. Incompetent. Pathetic. Useless. Worthless. Failure. Imposter. Incompetent.   Pathetic.   Useless.   Worthless. FailureImposterIncompetentPatheticUselessWorthlessFailureImposterIncompetentI

Forcing her racing mind and aching body to stop, Tessa leaned up against the wall. Placing her head on the cold plaster, she began to recite the alphabet in reverse under her breath. Slowly she calmed down, her heart slowed and her breathing normalised. The voices faded too. Tottering on her heels, Tessa took a step, a single faltering step, then another. Finally, she could manage a natural gait, breaking into a jog.

Lee had been waiting quietly in the foyer of the Agency, without being staff he could not go any further. Even companion demons were banned from the core of the Agency. Tessa bolted through the halls to tell him the news but skidded to a halt. A far too familiar stench assaulted her nose. Schimpf was sliming all over a water cooler, and an interaction with him would be the cherry on top of this shitty day. Tessa resolved to simply sneak by him. He almost let her escape into the foyer before oozing out into the hallway behind her.

'Well, well *Con-tessa*, I always knew you weren't up to this line of work,' he called after her, his greasy smile positively lighting up his doughy face.

'What do *you* want?' said Tessa, not even bothering to cover her disgust and annoyance. His grin widened as she took the bait.

'Well, a good agent would *never* let a witness become a poor victim of a *brutal* murder for all to see now, would they? Or let a trio of teens get torn apart?' Try as she might, Tessa could not stop the flashes of guilt darting back through her mind.

How did he know already?

She became even more annoyed at herself for letting slimy Schimpf get to her after all this time. He noticed her hesitation and jumped on it.

'Nothing to say huh? Let's hope the Agency can bury this particular story before it gets out, I wouldn't want all of the Agent's reputations damaged by your incompetence. At least if all else fails they can finally just fire you, *Con-tessa*' he practically spat the last words, his face contorting in hate.

'Look, I don't know why you hate me so, or what you think I did to you, but this attack was completely unforeseen. There is no way I could have known Skitch was going to be killed, or that those kids would... would... damn it.' Tessa was so upset now she was shouting, not caring who may be listening. Her voice cracked and tore as emotion took control.

Lee frowned as he heard how shrill she was getting, putting down his magazine and walking over to Tessa with quick strides.

'See? Look how unreasonable and uncontrollable you are. Women can never make good Agen...' Schimpf trailed off as Lee reached them, visibly going pale as the demon stood a head and a half taller than the now sweating man.

'Is there a problem doll?' Lee asked, casually throwing his arm around her shoulders. Schimpf's eyes almost boggled out of their sockets. Tessa shook her head and leant into Lee's embrace, understanding what he was doing. Normally Tessa would fight viciously to be able to stand up for herself without a man, but her emotions were still too raw. Schimpf would take this as validation that women were weak without men, but anything was needed to get rid of him today.

'Not really, just some pathetic attempt to undermine me as always. The usual arduous task with this degenerate really.' She had her control and thus her cynicism back with a vengeance. Redness crept into Schimpf's face as he began to splutter.

'You... and a demon? Professionalism... not allowed... protocol... management must know!' he finished, turning to run and tell on them like a small child. Of course, the pathetic little worm would make a beeline to management. Tessa grabbed his arm and threw him around, pushing him back into the alcove where the water dispenser was. A cold fury iced her veins.

'You dare do that and I will hunt you down and end you, you hear me? I have learnt a lot about torture from this job, and I can get reeeeal creative. You have no need for testicles, right?' The threat was barely a mutter, Tessa moving closer with each word until she was eyeball to eyeball with him.

He visibly shrank away as he backed down, nodding curtly as he took off through the foyer and out of the building. The stench slowly dissipated, as did Tessa's anger. Now Tessa felt oddly satisfied after standing up to her bully, but a worry gnawed at the back of her mind.

Why had she been so defensive of her sexual relationship with Lee? Plenty of other witches of all genders had done it before her. While Schimpf has stuttered about protocol, there really wasn't anything documented against fraternising with the demons because it was impossible to police. It certainly would not threaten her job.

So why was it making her so nervous? Eventually he would have to go back to Hel, and it would be by her own hand. The thought suddenly made her stomach turn.

Tessa found that she couldn't look Lee in the eyes, merely nodding and walking to the car for an equally silent ride home. Once she had settled in with a soothing cup of tea, she finally cracked open the report on the zombie attack, scanning it for anything useful. It was pretty much exactly how he had described; a small group of teens had entered the alley only to find it previously occupied by a group of stiffs. A few had been bitten and scratched but they had all managed to escape regardless. Luckily, they had the thought to work together, even dragging one of their companions out by their hair. The attack had been reported to the Agency rather late, when the kids had presumably dumped the drugs they were going to use.

A sweep and clean team had been sent out, but by the time they had gotten there the zombies had disappeared. All that was left was plenty of blood, hair and congealed gobbets of rancid flesh.

Forensics had found nothing of interest that would pertain to the case. Tessa sighed, sipping her tea. Who knows where else hidden enclaves of the shambling dead would be, waiting for some innocent to stumble across them.

She scanned the report one last time, until finally something jumped out at her. The alley in question was in a Western area of Bayton, and her previous theory solidified in her mind.

What if they had not been hiding out like a sleeper cell, but rather scoping out the alley for the next murder?

Perhaps the murderer sent her drones out before her in order to assess whether the murder site would be acceptable and quiet. Tessa grinned before jumping up and running to her bedroom, where Lee had stalked off to upon returning home. He was brooding again.

'I have a theory for you,' Tessa exclaimed, not bothering to knock in her haste. 'Read this, I think the dead weren't randomly there, in that alley. I think they were poking around for a good spot for their next murder. I was sure there is some weird cardinal points thing going on, and now they appear in West Bayton? I guess it helps with stealing the powers or whatever.' Lee nodded as she spoke, reading over the report which was now crumpled thanks to being in Tessa's possession for more than two minutes. She almost shook with excitement, hoping that this discovery could bring the case to an end.

'Yeah, I think you have a point. What are you going to do though?' he asked carefully, making Tessa suddenly stop and think. She had no real idea when the murderer would attack again, but seeing as the full moon was in a few nights time, she figured it wouldn't be long. Given that this was the magickal variety of nut-bag, she was sure they would take advantage of the power boost a full moon affords.

This was especially important as it seemed that the murderer was a woman, and thus closely bound to the moon's cycles. It would be an unmissable opportunity for her. Tessa doubted that the murderer would want to wait another whole month, given how desperately fast she was currently working.

'Well, I'm not sure actually. I am sure they are planning another attack, and I think it will be any time coming up to this full moon. I will call my supervisor and see if we can't get some help for surveillance or something, finally catch whoever this is while they are hunting. Maybe get some patrols going, looking for a redhead playing with the dead. She has to show up eventually if we just flood the streets there,' Tessa finished, drawing a deep breath after such a litany. Lee smiled weakly at her excitement but just nodded in response. She was already reaching for her phone anyway, not really waiting for him to speak in her rush to catch the killer.

There were only a few hours left of sunlight, and considering that every other murder had taken place at night, they had little time to organise patrols for the entire area of West Bayton tonight. Sir McAdams answered his mobile immediately, listened intently, and by the end of the call had a running roster of interns and hunters ready to patrol at sundown. All she had to do was wait until then to join them and together they would cover most of West Bayton until morning. Lee however, did not seem to share her euphoria at a possible solution of the case. Tessa finally noticed how quiet he had been for the whole afternoon.

'What's wrong? We are so close at last; we will finally stop this nutter and no one will be another victim,' Tessa asked, tilting her head to the side. He tried to smile, but it came out as a watery grimace.

'Well, I am so happy for you to be close to finishing up, catching the baddie and all that. But you know what happens then,' Tessa simply looked confused, so Lee sighed and continued.

'I get sent back to Hel,' he said flatly, dropping his eyes down as he said it. Tessa felt her world stop suddenly, struggling to even take a breath.

What was happening?

How had she not realised the effect it had on him? She had just assumed he was used to it as his role. Demons were often quite the afterthought for Agency witches, something she had always disliked, but now she was guilty of doing the same. Come to think of it, why *did* it affect her so much? It had only been a few days, but her heart ached at the idea, which filled her with fear.

Tessa simply stared at Lee, a thousand thoughts running through her mind, but none she could catch and vocalise.

'Hel...' was all she could get out before she began to choke up, suddenly feeling like the room was too big, too small, too... something. She sat down on the bed next to him numbly, just looking at him. Moments passed, the silence mounted before Lee finally and awkwardly broke it.

'Well that certainly was an awkward shocked silence thing. Very dramatic, so I appreciate the effort. It will be OK right?' He attempted levity, but refused to meet her eyes as he said it. Tessa sighed, trying to will herself to be able to say the right thing. She rehearsed half a dozen different things in her mind before blurting out the one that was taboo.

'But... I want you, here,' she said before clapping a hand over her mouth and blushing furiously. Lee looked startled, and Tessa instantly regretted her admission. 'I'm sorry, that was inappropriate... I shouldn't have... forget about it,' she trailed off lamely but Lee waved it off.

'Never in the long centuries I have been alive have I heard that and wanted to respond in kind.' Lee spoke formally, stiffly. Tessa simply stared and blinked for a few seconds, trying to comprehend if what he said was really what she had heard. Her brain seemed to rebel at the thought of such happiness. She even opened and closed her mouth a few times for good measure, but still, she could not get her frazzled mind to function. Finally, Lee simply pulled her into his arms, letting his body translate his words. Their lips met; sensuality bloomed between them.

Tessa deepened the kiss, grabbing the handful of hair at the back of his head and drawing him in. She moved to wrap her legs around him, locking them in place as he slid his hands under her shirt, running them up her back. He grasped the nape of her neck with one hand while with the other he simply tore her shirt away, buttons flying off to the far corners of the room. Tessa giggled and was about to point out the cost of clothing, but Lee chose that moment to gently run his nails down her back, eliciting an unfettered moan of satisfaction from her.

He put a hand on either side of her hips, pulling her forward until she could feel his hard erection pushing against her, pulsing with each beat of his heart. It took all of Tessa's self-control to stop herself from grinding against his hard on immediately, wanting to tease a little. Instead, she challenged him back, pulling cheekily at the handful of hair that she still had a hold of. She ran a trail of kisses down Lee's neck before nipping him gently on the small patch of chest revealed by his shirt. He growled in response, the tiny flare of pain merely heightening his arousal. His erection kicked and strained in his pants, begging to be released. Tessa answered its wishes, her nimble fingers popping the button and unzipping the fly in one movement. Her bra was deftly removed as she took him in her hands once more.

A fog of pleasure settled in Lee's mind, numbing his thoughts as he rained kisses on her breasts. He relished the sensation of their softness against his lips. The little witch had a perfect body to him, both soft and hard from well-trained muscles and a network of scars.

With her free hand Tessa gently touched the horns protruding from Lee's head, something she had wanted to do since he arrived. He seemed to feel it, smiling as he continued to devote his attention to her chest as his hands wandered. They were surprisingly smooth, each ridge running into the next. Running curious fingers all the way to the tip, Tessa was delighted with her findings.

Suddenly Lee stood up, taking her with him as if she weighed nothing at all. He stepped forward until Tessa's butt hit the window, pinning her gently to it. He kicked off his pants as he went and stood naked in all his glory. Her legs still wrapped around him, Lee pushed aside her underwear and buried himself deep within her.

'But... what if they see?' panted Tessa slowly, lost in the sensation of having him so intimately bound to her.

'Let them see. I want them to,' he growled, beginning to thrust within her. Tessa loved the thrill of exhibitionism and was endlessly thankful for security plate glass. Even the occasional squeak of sweaty flesh on glass couldn't ruin the mood.

They moved together as one, merging to become a single sweating, writhing, pleasure filled being. Magickal energy prickled between them, as the very core of their beings seemed to rise up with each stroke. She felt above herself, within herself, within him. Their separate energies came together, twisting around each other in an elegant dance. The pace quickened, spinning into a whirlwind of power. There were no longer two separate beings, two separate souls, just one maelstrom of witch and demon.

Tessa felt a connection snap into place between them, but the worry was torn away as she was caught up in the rush.

Shortly after Tessa felt the familiar pleasure rising, prickling up from her feet and building to a raging storm in her chest. Mere moments passed before it all unleashed and she came. Lee was only seconds behind her, having desperately held out as best he could. Seeing her in such pleasure, feeling her clench against him was too much to hold back. They stayed in that position, catching their breath and processing what had just happened.

'Did you just feel that?' asked Tessa, completely struck by what she had just experienced on a magickal level.

'Yeah... there's another first in four hundred years. Did our... magick... or souls... just merge too?' he replied with a question of his own. Tessa just nodded, feeling unable to respond. Breathless and sweaty, she revelled in both the pleasure and the magickal wonder she had just experienced.

Finally, she glanced guiltily over her shoulder to see what kind of audience they had through the now fogged and sweat soaked window.

Only Damien stood on the street below, looking up at them, his face twisted in anger. He looked almost inhuman, a man contorted by rage. His hands flexed angrily around a vodka bottle, which he cast off in fury when he saw Tessa looking down into the street.

'Oh no...' she gasped, dropping her legs to the floor and trying to steady herself on her own feet again.

'What... oh.' replied Lee flatly, as he saw what she had reacted to. He stepped away from her, unsure of what to do. Damien answered their unspoken question, storming off down an alleyway and into the night. An awkward silence descended as Tessa moved to sit on the bed, Lee joining her after he had closed the curtains.

Damien had been, up until recently, the closest man in her life. She had valued him. With the benefit of hindsight, she realised that she had even loved him in some way. But the man in that street was something bestial, transformed by her complete betrayal, seen tonight by his own eyes. It was no longer just a suspicion. Tessa knew that he had been hurting, but now she had destroyed anything between them. The high of the moment had well and truly passed now.

They sat in silence for quite some time before Tessa needed to break it for her own sanity.

'Sooo, soul sex huh?' she joked, knowing there was an uncomfortable amount of truth in what she had said. Lee nodded, relieved for the change of subject, even if it was a fairly forbidden one.

'I guess so Hel Cat, I guess so. That is something totally new to me, but it felt like an out of body thing. Something sacred. The only other time I felt anything similar was with some shamans about three hundred years ago, but that was... well enhanced with fly agaric.'

'Yeah, that is what it was like. I could feel us bind, and kind of inside each other. I still feel some kind of connection there.' she explained, chewing her lip in thought. Clearly this would require much more research. This was completely new, and she could feel that something energetically had changed between them.

His energy coursed through her, this wild tang of demon mingling with her innate witch magick.

Who knows what effects it may have?

Lee lay back on the bed, beckoning her into his arms. Tessa smiled and let him embrace her while she rested her head on his shoulder. They lay together, pondering the mysteries of their unusual relationship or sleeping off and on, without a word spoken.

There they lay naked until it was time to hunt a murderer.

The plan was to patrol the Western areas of Bayton as discreetly as possible, posing as lovers or drunken friends walking the streets and ducking into alleys for their role's various 'needs'. Every Agent that could be spared tonight was on patrol, some paired with disguised demons, others with fellow Agents, even the interns were let loose.

For Tessa and Lee, the lovers act was rather easy to ply. If they weren't out hunting a crazed murderess, they would have rather enjoyed the night. As it was their search proved fruitless, aside from busting a few dodgy types plying their trade. Another team had also caught the main suspect of another investigation in the act.

This happy coincidence had a few Agents positively beaming. A rogue witch was now being carted away, hollering curses to all around. It seemed that he was prone to attacking lovers in alleys and had gone after the wrong bait. Tessa had to wonder how the investigating Agent had not intercepted them sooner, however she had to fake a surprised reaction when she discovered that it was Schimpf. A snarky side of her considered that it was because he could not find someone to pose as his lover.

Overall Sir McAdams was happy enough, his cheeks flushed from a night of actually working and ideas of a regular patrol running through his head. Finally, an exhausted Tessa and Lee could return home to curl up together and sleep most of the day away.

Chapter Sixteen

When she awoke Tessa silently padded out to the kitchen, leaving Lee twitching away in his sleep. She made a beeline for her laptop to research the wonders of her current sex life. Even the afternoon after she could still feel the connection between them, feel every twitch of his restless sleep and could even feel the moment when his dream became a nightmare.

The internet failed to yield anything too useful, the closest she could find was some sketchy links to tantric sex. Even this didn't fit well with what she had experienced, so finally she just searched 'witch and demon magickal sex'. The barrage of well-illustrated pornographic media that existed in the online world was a shock to her.

Apparently, it was a popular subject.

Dredging through the muck revealed a small cache of anecdotes about such sexual encounters, all declaring they were a factual experience. She read through each of them in turn, but none mentioned anything to do with an encounter outside of the physical. They all seemed like rather awful works of fan-fiction, and Tessa suspected that was exactly what they were.

She sighed and shut down the tab, instead turning to study a map of the Western parts of Bayton, trying to guess where her murderous quarry would choose next. She marked off a few alleys of interest before succumbing to her restlessness and grabbed a light-hearted romance novel to while away the hours before the hunt.

Lee had all but given up on the idea of sleeping after hours of fitful napping. He had pretended to sleep as Tessa left the bed, preferring to be alone as his mind whirred over the events of the previous night. He hadn't been joking when he said this was the first time he had such an experience in all his life. When he had felt the depth of the connection that was made, he grew worried, bonds such as this were bad news when he had to return to Hel.

Not that it was a bad place mind you. It was merely an oblivion, spirits and demons coexisted without change. Like demons, Hel had just gotten a bad name over the years.

Regardless, return he must, and this connection to Tessa would make it difficult. Lee already couldn't imagine being without her, but as an immortal that was a given. Demons weren't allowed to fraternise beyond sexual dalliances, and it really was for their own mental health. The tales of demons gone bad due to pining over a lost love abounded in Hel, told in the same warning tones as fairy tales once had. Just a hint of emotion was enough to make for horror stories around the proverbial campfires back home.

It was something he had always found relatively easy to adhere to, although in four hundred years he had never felt such a lure as he had to this woman. He ached to see it through, allow himself to love her wholly and purely. He sighed, idly scratching around his horns, where last night she had touched him so curiously.

As he lay there, he realised that he could feel every emotion of hers, even down to the arousal she felt upon reaching a lusty scene in her book. That was terribly distracting, and when his body began to react also, Lee finally gave up the idea of sleeping.

Tessa looked up from her book as Lee surfaced looking sleepy and worried. With his hair all tousled and pants creased from sleep, Lee looked more human than ever. This delusion of normalcy was so painfully fleeting. Her heart skipped a beat as he sat on the couch beside Tessa, so she put her book aside.

'So, Hel Cat, what shall we do?' Lee asked, leaving 'about these feelings' unsaid.

'Well,' started Tessa. 'I would settle for a date!' A smile bloomed across Lee's face. Somehow, she had managed to bypass all the awkwardness with her cheeky suggestion.

'How about we do just that? Let's do it! Tonight!' he exclaimed, jumping out of his seat. Tessa laughed at his exuberance, feeling happier for the first time in days.

'But the patrol?' Tessa queried as Lee dragged her up to hold in his arms.

'We have a few hours before we have to be there, and we can go straight over,' Lee said, checking his watch.

'But that means I have to wear sensible shoes,' Tessa whined, as Lee looked dubiously at the sky-high heels Tessa usually wore to work, kicked off by the door.

'As opposed to?' Lee asked cheekily, giving her a gentle push in the direction of the room. Tessa obliged, quickly showering and dressing. She opted for a roomy circle skirt and blouse, just in case she needed to do some running while on patrol. Strapping on some low Mary-Janes, Tessa applied a little make up and stepped out.

Lee had also managed a quick change, now dressed in black pants, a button-down shirt and a blood red motorcycle jacket. Tessa had no idea where he kept pulling these clothes from, but she definitely approved. His hair had been slicked back again, his horns proudly on display. She hooked her arm in his, threw her bag over her shoulder and they waltzed out the door, giggling all the way.

After a quick debate in the car, they decided on a quirky diner which sold pizza by the slice with excessively fancy milkshakes. Sitting in a booth seat overlooking a busy dance floor, Tessa smiled at the normalcy of the date. Aside from the horns, they could be any young couple in Bayton. From the stares of other patrons, they were clearly not passing so well, however. People on the dance floor kept stopping to gawk, so Tessa finally just turned her back to them. Lee just smiled, delighted at the candy on top of his milkshake.

'What's wrong Tessa? You look worried,' he stated, picking up another greasy slice of mushroom pizza with delight. The new foods of this time certainly appealed to him, especially when they mirrored the last time he was summoned, the 1950's. There were many vast improvements of course, present company included.

'Just feeling... well you know, this is all so normal, but it's not. Hah, I haven't been on an official date like this in years.' Tessa sighed, wishing that somehow she could form the thoughts in her head into coherent sentences. Lee laughed heartily.

'I win! It has been at least five decades, no seven DECADES, since I have eaten out on a date like this with, well, anyone really,' he said, bemused at the thought.

Had it really been so long?

Time flew when you wintered in Hel.

'Woah that is going to take some getting used to,' mused Tessa, thinking of their considerable age gap. Lee grinned and gave a cheeky look.

'Oh, so you plan on getting used to me huh?' he asked mischievously. Tessa blushed furiously at the implication of his words, well aware that it was a complete taboo. That word kept running through her mind, reminding her to be guarded.

'Uhhh, well I mean... for this case, you know. It's nice to have such good company this time round,' she finished lamely, awkwardly sipping on her milkshake and staring down at the colourful sprinkles adorning a bobbing chunk of whipped cream. She pretended to be very interested in poking it around with her straw, sinking the chocolate bar in the milkshake under the froth.

The heat in her face was finally dying down. Lee let her go on that one, seeing how uncomfortable this conversation made her. Truth be told, he had no idea what to say. They finished eating in relative silence, only speaking to share sips of each other's shakes and comment on the dancers. Eventually it became a comfortable silence, both parties happy to just be in each other's presence.

Tessa groaned loudly when the alarm went off on her phone, signalling that it was time to head back to work. They paid the bill and dutifully trooped out to go on patrol.

Chapter Seventeen

The streets of West Bayton were cold and wet as the various members of the Agency on patrol shivered their way through the debriefing. Tessa had passed on the details of the alleys she had identified as being of particular interest to the group, then turned them loose. Again, the small army of drunks and lovers spread out, investigating every alley and den to prevent another death. Many of them had heard about the handiwork of the crazed red head and were desperate to not have another victim subjected to that torture.

Tessa and Lee patrolled together, searching both physically and magickally. Aside from the occasional sex spell or appearance glamour, it proved fruitless. It felt as though they were just wandering around for no point. Tessa could feel her frustration rising uncontrollably. They had only two days left before this murderer had enough mojo to do whatever the Hel she was doing. Time was running out. Each turn she made through the labyrinthine network of alleys that made up Western Bayton only served to increase her fear of failure.

At one point they bumped into Tessa's rival from the markets, the decrepit woman seeming to find something inherently funny in the entire situation. While Tessa still itched to slap her for stealing her stall, she had to be mature and settle for hitching her nose in the air and flouncing by. This of course merely made the woman cackle louder, but Tessa could not waste time on petty squabbles. Instead, she forced herself to resume the search, checking the time. It was 4.32am, and the sun would be up in a matter of hours. It looked like another futile endeavour.

Barely a quarter of an hour had passed before a shout rang out, and a panicked call came out over the Agency radios. An actual *hoard* of zombies had appeared, and it was all hands on deck to deal with them. For mere seconds Tessa got to appreciate how much like a B-grade horror film her life had become. After the moment of indulgence had passed, she cued Lee in and bolted over to the battle zone, a few streets over from where they currently were. They could already hear the shouts and a few screams, so they hastened their pace. Tessa tossed Lee half of the vials they had made up to act as little zombie stopping spell grenades, with an unspoken understanding of how this would go down.

As they rounded the corner the true extent of their situation hit them. A group of around forty zombies were gathered around two of their Agents, while the others frantically and impotently tried to fight their way in from the outskirts. Apparently only Tessa and Lee had thought to come prepared with spells, the first of which Tessa threw at the nearest group of walking corpses. As it broke green powder puffed out, and the zombies it came into contact with instantly dropped, their un-life banished by a potent mix of ajenjible, sloe and sage.

'Green powder works a treat!' Tessa shouted to Lee as she spun a nearby zombie around, embedding her knife blade into the base of its skull. The other Agents began to follow her lead and stopped merely battering at them, in favour of decapitation and its variants.

Lee kicked away a corpse so rotted it was hard to tell if it had once been male or female, flinching as it fell to the floor with a sickening crack of bone breaking. He threw a vial of pink liquid, designed to lock dead flesh in place and prevent it moving, but the genderless zombie and those around it were still advancing.

'Pink doesn't work, I told you I didn't like the idea of the pink one!' He said, throwing a green one instead. Tessa dumped the pink vials that she had before burying her dagger in the eye of a rather obese male zombie and threw a blue powder vial into the fray. The target zombie and those around it stopped suddenly, seeming confused, before beginning to shuffle around in a random manner. The blue powder was designed to block the bond of the corpse to its controller, and it seemed to work well.

'Blue works, and it might help us track the magickal link back,' Tessa announced, rather happy by that revelation. They were working their way through the crowd well now, almost up to the trapped Agents. The two were still fighting, but as Tessa watched the female Agent fell, pulled into waiting hands. Before anyone could help her, the mass fell upon her, and instantly her screams became gurgled wails, lost to the blood falling freely from her mouth. The other zombies became distracted by the promise of easy flesh and toddled over for a bite.

Tessa threw a green mix onto the feeding frenzy, watched it break over the body of the fallen Agent. The puffs of green instantly dropped the nearest shamblers. The next lot who came forward also dropped, so it appeared that the spell also worked when consumed with flesh.

Not really willing to ponder the implications of the fact she had just used the body of a co-worker as bait, Tessa launched herself furiously at the nearest zombie and tackled it to the ground. Almost severing its head, she furiously cut its spinal cord and jumped up, throwing another blue vial. Lee fought by her side, alternating between throwing spell vials and breaking necks.

Together they fought through the rest of the crowd, making it to the surviving Agent. He was badly bitten but still standing, and better yet, still fighting. They grabbed him under each arm and with the backup of the other Agents, limped him to safety. The medics rushed over to help, having finally arrived. Luckily, someone had foresight enough to call for medical support when the scuffle started.

All that was left was about five zombies, still very intent on maiming any Agent in reach. They were dispensed of with the last of Tessa's vials, which she handed out to the other Agents. Working together, they fetched the disconnected zombies, herding them into a flock like sheep in order to shackle them together. Without their mistress's murderous intent, they were actually rather docile, and Tessa hoped they would provide something to trace back to the red headed witch. Sir McAdams was fluffing around and had soon gathered the group together for some kind of pompous announcement.

'Well, a sorry night and a sorry loss. It seems only Lady Bale and her demon had come prepared, and thus saved the day because of it.' The gathered Agents coughed and shuffled, none too willing to point out that the self-important fool had not been prepared either. He was the Agent responsible for their employment after all.

'Tomorrow shall be a day of mourning for our fallen Agent, and I shall personally notify the family. I thank you all for your... eh? Whassat?' he muttered, digging through his jacket pocket as an alarm blared from it. He pulled out his phone and answered it tersely, suddenly going very pale. The conversation appeared to be mostly nods and grimaces, causing Tessa and Lee to exchange glances and shrugs. Sir McAdams snapped his phone closed and drew them both aside, waving to shoo the other Agents away.

'During the foray... another murder... right under our noses,' he spoke in a barely contained whisper, repeatedly running a hand through his hair and developing a decidedly sweaty sheen.

'WHAT? Where? When?' exclaimed Tessa, looking frantically at Lee. They may have been too late now, the four cardinal points had probably been completed. Sir McAdams began to wring his hands.

'A few streets over, a bum...erm man, called it in after losing a hard-earned meal when he found the body. Called from a phone booth over on Kerree Lane. Apparently, the body was still warm, the sad creature tripped over it.'

Tessa slumped slightly, her shoulders falling as her mood darkened. 'We were assigned that area. We investigated it at the start of the night and were about to patrol back there when we got the call that the mass had attacked. Caryn and Aidyn were patrolling the other end of the alley, but I guess they ran straight here too, they were here before we were. Should we head over?' she asked, feeling consumed by dejection now that the night had turned so dark.

'Yes, I shall excuse you from the clean-up in order to pursue the investigation. Go to,' he commanded arrogantly before waving a hand at them and turning back to the other Agents.

The body was there all right, but barely recognisable as anything other than human and probably Caucasian. The sigils were carved in so deep that muscle and bone showed in most areas. Those that were burnt in had been done to the point of blackening the skin around the brand. The body was indeed still warm, although the cool night was seeing to that fast. Tessa wasted no time in sending out feelers for magick, feeling a frail line of it disappearing down the alley. The residue was dispersing but was still strong enough to be a trail.

Tessa looked to Lee, trying to determine whether she should follow the trail or investigate the body. He nodded at her and Tessa ran, leaving Lee with the body to take pictures and have a look over it. The trail of magick felt acrid and ill, akin to a sour fruit. Tessa drew it in, memorising its signature and unique style. The owner was definitely losing sanity, a chaos pulsing through the magick with no control to speak of.

The trail twisted and turned, going north and slowly getting stronger. She was finally gaining on it, although her burning lungs and legs had forced her to slow a little. Tessa just hoped that the murderess would be unaware that she was being followed and stop somewhere to hide. She kept jogging onwards, still going towards the northern areas, towards her house, or more to the point, the market.

With a group of people that large and with so much conflicting magick it would be hard to follow the trail. If the witch disappeared into there Tessa would be severely hampered in her efforts to track her. Praying frantically that the witch avoided the crowds, Tessa was forced to slow her pace to a fast walk in her exhaustion. Sure enough, the magickal trail turned off into the busy market and dispersed completely. She huffed angrily.

Tessa strode into the crowd, following what she hoped was shreds of the magickal trail. The bitter taste of the rogue magick was there but she just couldn't get a sure path on where it went. In frustration she kicked at a nearby bin. She stalked around the food stalls, just trying to pick up something in passing, but it seemed like her natural luck had abandoned her. All she found was mud, desperation and that stench that never seems to leave the slum areas. A more poetic person may note that the stench clings to the skin of those entrenched in the mire, or leeched into their souls, but Tessa was beyond poetic. Her frustrated gaze simply slipped over the usual crowd, grime and little flashes of spellwork hidden in the crevices of the Central Bayton region.

Perhaps the red headed witch had already left, gone to some little bolt hole with her stash of stolen magick, like a petulant raccoon. Perhaps it was all over, and Tessa would just have to wait to see what wicked deed would now wreak havoc on Bayton.

Tessa toyed with the idea of trying to talk to Damien about it but quickly abandoned that poor choice. It really was not worth it. She strongly doubted that he would ever talk to her again, given the feeling of betrayal and animosity that stretched between them. He may know all the coming and goings of the Central Bayton area, but this resource was definitely tapped out. He had replaced her in every way possible.

Speaking of, it occurred to Tessa that the hideous creature who stole her stall couldn't be working tonight, given that she was lurking around West Bayton less than an hour ago. However, when Tessa went to go check out who had her stall now, the familiar toothless grin of the woman beamed back at her. Tessa scowled at her, her stall and the ugly little magickal items she sold. Their magick was fairly weak, a tiny pulse coming from each item. Tessa pressed her own power into them, neutralising the magick in the items in a petty little tiff. The woman didn't react, even if she did know what Tessa was doing she just smiled on vacantly.

Even playing with the items left a bad taste in Tessa's mouth, but its only when she touched her market rival with a magickal feeler that she made the connection. The woman felt acrid and ill, akin to a sour fruit. It was a magickal signature that she had memorised, kept safe in her core and treasured, the signal of the murderess. The old hag was the red headed zombie queen.

Tessa jumped in shock and the market rival come murderess finally reacted, having sensed Tessa's intrusion. She hissed and turned on her heel, bolting down an alleyway behind her stall. Tessa ran after her, familiar with the network of lanes and alleys in this area from working here for so long. She dug out her phone, hammering in the number for Sir McAdams.

'Lady Bale, I...'

'I know who it is!' explained Tessa, panting from too much exertion. The hag from the market moved surprisingly quickly, soon becoming just a heel or piece of hair disappearing around a corner.

'There is a woman with a stall at the market in Central Bayton, she has the same magickal signature. I know it is he- oof!' Tessa stopped short as she was suddenly hit in the face by someone from an unseen doorway. She was vaguely aware of the voice that was now shouting at her from the phone as she sank to the floor and everything went black.

Chapter Eighteen

When she came to Tessa was in the standard abduction room, dimly lit, bound hands and feet, however this one was filled with the most disgusting stench. It was sewerage and mould, with strong undertones of death. Half of her face was crusted with the dirt from the wretched alley floor she had passed out upon. She tried wiping it on her shoulder, only to realise that shoulder was coated in something wet but chunky. Looking down, she was aghast to realise that it was a good dose of raw sewerage. Wherever she was, whatever had happened to her, it involved a nice varied blend of human waste.

She started gagging immediately, which attracted the attention of the red headed witch. She stalked over, all remnants of the decrepit and gnarled crone now gone in favour of a delicate, pale auburn beauty. She was tall, well dressed and unkempt. Her hair was tufted out at odd angles, and she had badly chipped nail polish on chewed nails.

Despite her beauty, the woman was dishevelled and had an aura of feralness. Clearly sanity had not been a friend to her of late.

'Hello, bitch,' she drawled, a slight but unrecognisable accent tainting her vowels.

'Well let's just do away with all the pleasantries you psycho,' responded Tessa, trying to shake off the wooziness and assess how shattered her nose was. As she raised her head, she could feel blood clots sliding down the back of her throat. Her stomach boiled in disgust, but she held it all down, glaring at her rival.

'Hah! Still feisty despite having your nose splattered across your face. I would almost like you if you weren't completely putting my plans at risk. Still, you gotta go I'm afraid,' rambled the woman, tapping a finger on her chin vacantly. The fact that she mirrored Tessa's own habits was unnerving. Tessa scowled up at her some more, being the most she could do for now.

'Your plans huh? Some nutty murderous stuff to get a zombie army? Yeah that's a real brilliant one there. Whatcha gonna do, take over the world?' she taunted, practically spitting on each word. The other witch just sighed. She almost looked disappointed at Tessa's suggestion.

'You are so far off base. I can't imagine you could possibly understand something like love would you? True love, the kind that ensnares you and enchants you and feeds your soul. The kind you would kill for or be killed by. No, you are just some pathetic Agency lap dog.' shouted the witch, spitting back. Tessa thought on the matter. Assuming she could get away, that was probably a good hint. Plus, the woman clearly riled up fast. This was also useful information.

'So what, you're going to kill me huh?' asked Tessa sweetly. The red head paced irately, twirling part of her scruffy hair around her shaking fingers.

'Well, you see I can't, not without stuffing up the flow of magick. That's the real kicker. But honestly, I don't even like the killing. It just has to happen. And those icky hands... ugh. I mean dead bodies are just so nasty.'

'But you do it so well,' smirked Tessa, practically feeling the crazy tainting the air around this woman.

'Only because it is the only thing that will work,' replied the other witch, now reverting to tapping on her chin. Clearly, she was a poster child for vagueness and nervous tics.

'Well if you are not going to do the spill the plan to the hero who is about to die thing, will you at least tell me your name? I prefer to know whose name to take with me to Hel.' Tessa was willing to try anything to both delay and get more information from the hot but murderous red head. Interestingly enough, this request almost seemed to entertain her, a musical laugh bursting from her perfectly pink lips.

'I suppose there is no harm in you knowing my name. Might as well be on a first name basis with the one who has hunted me so well. I am Ramona, and while your silly Agency tests missed my skills, I am very grateful for it now. I don't really want to know your name. It's rather irrelevant to me,' she stated, still giggling in odd fits like a little girl. The effect was fairly unnerving, which was either the intent, or entirely incidental.

'Well Ramona, lovely to meet you, too bad you are just another nut-bag serial killer.' Tessa was trying to wind Ramona up into making a mistake. But the murderess merely smiled, slapped Tessa across the face and stalked over to a small shopping bag.

Tessa choked and sneezed as her nose started bleeding again, spraying herself with blood and clots. Ramona turned back towards her with a handful of duct tape rolls.

'Ugh, gross. You are really disgusting, you know that?' she sneered, a look of utter distaste marring her perfect features. Tessa simply smiled and sniffed loudly and wetly, trying to irritate Ramona further.

'That is a hell of an accent you managed to put on as a vile old hag. You almost sound educated. Now.' Tessa stumbled over her words slightly due to the blocked and bleeding nose. Ramona smiled widely, clearly thrilled at the compliment given.

"Yes, wasn't it? Maybe after all this I can go into a career as an actress, when I have...' Ramona trailed off, stopping tantalisingly close to revealing a clue. 'Well, speaking of which, given what I have learnt from so many movies, I can't just tie you up with rope and leave you for some kind of miracle escape, but I also can't just straight up kill you. So, its duct tape mummy and a rather precarious situation involving a sewer pipe I'm afraid. I won't be too much more creative, because Hel, it's a sewer and no one knows you're here! But don't worry, I will leave you with a small army to make sure you aren't disturbed.' Ramona smiled in a twisted manner, a brilliant flash of her insanity showing.

She wasn't joking when she mentioned mummies, binding Tessa from the chin to her toes in layers of the tape. When she was done Tessa was rendered immobile by a rigid cocoon. She stepped back to admire her handiwork before dragging Tessa and the flimsy fold up chair to a gutter down the side of the room, positioning them beneath an open pipe.

'I assume this gets flushed regularly or something, every time I come here it is wet. So good luck with that. I have a lot of stuff to get ready for my little fiesta, so I will have to love you and leave you my dear.' Suddenly the visage of the beautiful woman vanished, replaced by the ugly hag once more. She blew a rotting kiss at Tessa before picking up the bag and skipping out of the only door to the room. Assuming she could get out of a cocoon that was literally stuck to her skin, the only way out was either through that door or up the sewer pipe. Neither seemed to be a viable option currently.

Tessa strongly doubted that Ramona had made an idle threat about the zombies, she did seem to have plenty of them at her disposal. Soon enough there was a flurry of loud shuffling which slowed to a stop, followed by the creeping stench of death overwhelming the room. Her guard of honour had clearly arrived and gotten into position.

Initially Tessa tried struggling, but she was stuck fast, as was the general idea with tape. All she did was exhaust herself and pull out every one of the little hairs on her skin. She pondered calling for help, screaming until her throat was raw, but given where she was and her guests out the front door, it was unlikely anyone would get to her alive. In her dark little heart, Tessa knew that if someone died while trying to save her, the screaming damsel in distress, she could never forgive herself. She tried to lever an arm out, hoping to get to the small utility knife in her bra, but Ramona sure knew how to play mummies. For now, all Tessa could do was wait and hope that this pipe was not going to be flushed any time soon.

Chapter Nineteen

Time crawled by until finally Tessa simply resorted to just screaming in frustration. It was so unfair for her to die like this when things were finally going well. She had work, she had her rat hole apartment, and now she had Lee in her life. In this moment, Tessa had to admit he had changed her life for the better and become a part of it. Heck, he was now a part of her. She internally kicked herself for only realising it in a life and death situation.

Tessa was in love with Lee.

The ultimate taboo for a witch and a demon. *Especially* an Agency witch. Sex was fine, but love, love was forbidden. Tessa sat there in silence, letting that little realisation sink in. She could never tell him. Never. She would have to return him to Hel and her normal life would have to go on. There was no way this little fantasy could play out.

The pipe above her head gurgled ominously, interrupting her thoughts and making her thankful that at least she could take that little gem to her grave. When several long minutes ticked by and nothing happened, Tessa released the breath she had been holding. The imagined gush of foul water to end her days never came. Barely even a drip was emitted from the pipe. The nose searing stench spewing from the pipe certainly gave her an idea of what her death may smell like at least.

Tessa sighed and resumed her fidgeting, wiggling her fingers and toes to stave off the pins and needles that were setting in. She thought back to all that had led her to this point, and she was certainly unwilling to die at only twenty two. Even though her childhood had been some kind of experiment in psychological resilience, Tessa realised that she would be leaving her parents behind, childless and neurotic. Friends were few and far between, but she still had a few old acquaintances that she wished she had stayed in contact with. Then there was Lee. Presumably he would be dragged back to Hel the second she died, since his living link to the world was gone.

Overall, this definitely did not fit her ideal life plan. To be fair, nothing from the last few weeks had been what Tessa expected from life, but this was definitely sub-par. Death by the faecal matter and flushed contraband of Bayton. Oh joy. That was if the water even killed her. The alternative didn't seem much of an improvement.

Just when she was beginning to contemplate dying of thirst, hunger or septicaemia down there instead, a warm sensation came over her. Someone very familiar was nearby, someone she knew intimately. She didn't know how she knew it, but Lee was coming. That, or she had already lost her marbles and was hallucinating. Actually, that was more likely given that no one knew she was here. Nor could they track her scent, as the smell of sewerage still burnt her nose. Perhaps a fever was setting in already from the festering bacteria in this sewer. Yeah, it was definitely a febrile hallucination.

Outside the shuffling came alive again, followed by some heavy thuds and the sound of glass smashing. Determined that she was hallucinating, Tessa refused to believe she was being rescued until the flimsy tin door burst open under the pressure of a very heavy boot. Her heart leapt as Lee strode into the room, a green powder vial ready in one hand and a bloody knife in the other.

'Lee!! That damn bitch who stole my stall is the killer! Her name is Ramona and... ohhhh get me outta here, it stinks so bad,' she finished pleading, not wanting to be stuck there any longer. Tear stained, mascara streaked, with most of her red locks caught in the tape housing her shaking body, Tessa was acutely aware that this was not her greatest moment. Lee smiled and nodded, stuffing the vial into his back pocket before hauling her gently out of the gutter.

'Blegh, you sure do stink there Hel Cat,' he teased, wrinkling his nose. Tessa grimaced, slightly embarrassed by the smell. Lee used his knife to delicately and carefully cut her loose. Soon she was up and about, sorely lacking the hairs on any exposed flesh and gently feeling her smashed nose. She carefully coaxed it back into place, resigning herself to the fact that she would have raccoon eyes for a while. Lee cupped her face in his hands, checking on her nose himself.

'That witch sure made a mess of you my dear, but I think you have gotten it mostly in place. Here, have some water to wash out the clots. I am guessing you had a few there.' Tessa nodded, gratefully accepting the offered water bottle and gulping down half before using the rest to clean her face and neck of blood.

'How did you find me?' asked Tessa, confused but so very thankful.

'I knew you were in a sewer from your reactions to it all, then I got a rough idea where you were magickally. The rest? Well, I just looked for the most walking deadies. I told you, I always know where you are.' Lee spoke with another earnest look on his face. They stood awkwardly for a few seconds, just looking at each other before Lee nodded and began to lead the way back out. Tessa hesitated.

'Hey Lee?' she queried timidly. Now was her chance to tell him the truth. Now was her moment. He turned back to look at her, head cocked and listening.'I, um, was really scared and I thought I was gonna die. Yeah, and um thanks.' she stammered, deciding at the last minute to keep her little revelation to herself. Lee simply nodded courteously and stepped out to guide the way to freedom.

As much as Tessa wanted to immediately go scouring the streets for Ramona, Lee insisted she bathe first and check in with Sir McAdams. He had already been notified that she was safe by Lee, but demanded to speak to her as soon as she was physically able to. Tessa had never appreciated any shower quite so much as that one, scrubbing away the smell of the sewer. The sticky residue from the tape was harder to remove, and the memories were probably going to provide her with nightmare fuel for the rest of her life..

While Sir McAdams seemed relieved to hear from her, he rather quickly brought up the new murder.

'Lady Bale, this latest event is of great embarrassment to the Agency. Not only has someone been murdered while we had pretty much every Agent on duty in the area, but she is a pain in the ass to us. Some spoilt brat with a trust fund from Upton decided it would be fun to be a pro- erm, sex worker for a while. So, the drug addled brat bites it, and the family is riding my ass to do something about it. The sprout's father plays golf or hide the chorizo with the mayor or something, now my job is up shit creek,' he ranted, clearly not caring to choose his words right now.

'Um, Sir?' Tessa intervened, shocked at what he was saying. The man was a pig, but even so, this seemed extreme.

'Oh yes, sorry. I haven't slept yet. Ahem. The victim is one Tasha Lane, no fixed address. She has been living out of the family home for three months now. We have been unable to ascertain if there was a boyfriend or even friends at all here in Bayton. Clearly, she didn't call home much.' Sir McAdams had to stop and have a wheeze before continuing. 'So, she must have been made from tougher material than the last woman. As I am sure you are aware, the spell appears to be successful. Now you say you know who this is Lady Bale?' he asked, hinting that she had better have answers for him. Tessa sighed with exhaustion.

'Yes Sir. She is a woman called Ramona. Red hair. I need all the information about any woman matching that description you can dig up in either Bayton or Upton. I suspect she comes from either city. Perhaps the mundane systems will be useful too, as she said she was missed by the Agency testing', reported Tessa in a nasal tone that sounded bratty, thanks to her injuries.

'I see, any more information you could give me? It will be hard to narrow that down to the 700,000 people in Bayton alone.' As much as it irritated Tessa, he was correct. Red headed Ramona was not enough to go on.

'Let's see, Tall, maybe five foot ten, slender. Oh, greenish eyes too. Slight accent but not enough to tell where it's from. I don't remember any tattoos but she did have a small birth mark on the back of her left hand. I saw it as she was slapping me in the face with that hand. Heh,' Tessa smirked, still feeling the pain from her nose. The delicate skin around her eyes was already turning a deep purple.

'Oh, erm, yes, well. I shall get the Agency files pulled and contact the mundane police for information. Depending on them I should have it by tomorrow afternoon. Hmm I will get that daft intern to dig through the Agency testing records too. What's his name?' Sir McAdams was beginning to sound confused again, so he had to be feeling better.

'You mean Scottie? He stuck around after the tongue incident?' Tessa asked, eliciting a chuckle from Sir McAdams.

'Apparently. Kid must be determined. Perhaps I should assign you to be his field work mentor, give him a good test. Ah, I must go, the lawyers from Ms Lane's family are back. God-damn...' Sir McAdams promptly hung up the phone. Tessa sat a moment to think.

A murder occurring while the Agency patrolled the area was highly embarrassing and jobs along with respect may be lost as a result. She just had to hope that it wasn't hers. Tessa really had no idea of what else she may do for employment if she did lose her job so soon after stepping out of her internship. She had never really been a ten-year plan kinda gal, but this was too risky.

Lee had been pacing the room like a caged wolf since they had gotten home, seeming angry but thoughtful. Every now and then he scratched his horns or stroked his chin, but he never ceased his pacing. When Tessa got off the phone the barrage of questions started.

'So, what did he say?'

'Well, the latest kid was from a rich family from the trendy part of Upton. The lawyers are grinding Sir McAdams, so he is grinding me,' Tessa replied, flopping down onto the couch.

'Lawyers? From the victim?" he asked, cocking his head in confusion. Tessa nodded, remembering that he had not been summoned since the 1950's.

"It is starting to be standard practice. If you are rich enough you pay your lawyer to hassle law enforcement, so they are forced to drop everything to pursue the one case. The fear of negative press always works well. It is a little annoying, but I guess they have the money to be annoying," Tessa quipped as Lee snorted with morbid laughter.

"So, we have to shift it. Got it. What next?"

"Well if you remember where that sewer room is, I guess we had better check it out tomorrow. In the evening, we will have to case out the market and see if that bitch... witch Ramona returns for another shift. Those are probably our best bets right now. The mundane cops will probably take at least a day to get back with their info on Ramona. Forensics for Tasha should come in tomorrow too but I am pretty sure there won't be anything new. Just another little baggie of evil and plenty of carving." Tessa went quiet for a moment as she tried to think of a plan. "You know, I am really tired and freaked out right now. Thanks for not letting me go running out for revenge Lee. I doubt I would have made it to the next block," Tessa spoke apologetically, realising that he understood her far more than she understood herself at times. She felt exhausted now that the rush of being abducted and subsequently rescued had worn off. Her body had chewed through the adrenalin and was now crashing badly.

Yawning and rubbing her burning eyes, Tessa allowed Lee to walk her to the bedroom. He even undressed her, put her snuggliest pyjamas on and tucked her into bed. As she slumbered he gazed at her tired face. His little hellion looked so serene now.

He had been paralysed with fear when Sir McAdams had waddled up to the crime scene, shouting about a phone call, a thump and finally managing to communicate that Tessa had been potentially taken by the murderer. Time seemed to slow, an icy shock ran through his chest as he begged Sir McAdams to give him more information. It had been pure blind panic, a savage thing. The severity of his reaction had worried him as much then as it did now. This was more than just the standard concern for his summoning witch. He lay down beside her, just as exhausted from many long hours of searching for Tessa.

Chapter Twenty

Together they slept for the rest of the day and that night. In the early hours of the morning Lee finally woke, and gently extracted himself from Tessa's arms. She simply murmured to herself and slept on peacefully. He sat in the lounge room window and watched the sun rise. It was a brief moment of peace in his life, and it was precious. He felt much better after such a long sleep, and just a little emotionally recharged. Little things like watching the sun rise and colours flood the sky made his time in Hel more bearable. Other demons loved the job, the travelling and constant new situations. Lee had always found it to be tiresome and felt as though he rarely fit in with his own kind. These humans, with their vibrant but short lives felt far more akin to him. It was their vibrancy that he adored, revelled in when he got his slivers of respite.

Today the search for this Ramona would begin in earnest, with what small information they had. Catch a murderer with only her first name, which she could be lying about, with a description of her appearance that she could easily disguise.

Simple.

No problem.

Lee gave a wry chuckle. The first time topside in sixty odd years and the case was a living nightmare. Then he would have to return to Hel and try to get over the one witch that he had fallen for in four hundred years of existence. Perhaps they had a "Pathetic Lovestruck Demons" self-help group in Hel for other miserable bastards like him. Unlikely though, most stuck to the rules, or seemed rather heartless.

Just when he was beginning to truly wallow in his own morose ponderings, Tessa made a yawning, snorting appearance. He was truly delighted at the interruption, happy to be able to ignore his pendulous thoughts.

She zombie shuffled directly to the kettle and its warm promise of caffeinated joy. Lee smiled and let her be, content to watch her stumble around the kitchen, cussing out inanimate objects. Eventually she came bearing coffee and handed him one. The silence was awkward, broken only by desperate slurps of their respective drinks. Neither witch nor demon was game to speak up about their worries.

In due time they both showered and dressed. Tessa was coated in concealer in an attempt to cover up her black and blue raccoon eyes. Lee had managed to find the room in the sewer that Tessa had been interred in and marked it on a map of the tunnels. As much as she never wanted to go back there again, she was obligated to meet the forensic team there and at least take a look for any clues that Ramona may have left behind.

They called in the location that the team would be needed in, then Tessa booted up with the oldest and most watertight boots she owned. Her pretty Mary-Janes from the previous night had been completely ruined. They were already tossed into the outside dumpster, after their stench had pervaded the entire apartment, resulting in their banishment. Resigned to the fact that they had to spend the morning in a sewer looking for anything unusual, they begrudgingly headed out.

The sewer maze was easily traversed with the help of an eager employee of the waste disposal services. He had been ecstatic to be involved in an active investigation, telling them both about his intense passion for crime novels. They were followed by a very unhappy forensics team, three miserable and slightly green faces trudging through the muck. The room was exactly as small and fetid as Tessa remembered. Carefully they collected up all the pieces of duct tape that had bound Tessa. The forensic technicians explained that they could sometimes find fingerprints preserved in the adhesive.

This sparked a new interest in searching every inch of that room and the hallway preceding it, just in case there was some other unlikely piece of evidence. It was Lee who managed to spot a balled up piece of paper in a gutter running along the hallway. It was photographed and carefully retrieved. The lead forensics technician carefully opened it back out, gently smoothing the most crumpled areas. It was a receipt for a local hardware store for five rolls of duct tape and a shovel. It was far too much of a coincidence that more than one person in that particular sewer had been purchasing so much tape. It had to be from Ramona. They carefully read it but unfortunately, she had paid in cash, so there was no credit trail.

The slip of paper was dusted for fingerprints, but unfortunately there was only large oily smudges, no clear prints. After the receipt was bagged and labelled they continued searching but found nothing more aside from the zombies Lee had disposed of. Some poor mortuary assistant had a rather large meat jigsaw puzzle to be solving. They left the various zombie parts for the technicians to pick up, stating that they urgently needed to go do some research. Tessa and Lee practically ran the entire way to the surface, gulping in big lungfuls of air in the cleansing sunshine.

They had intended to go to the Agency and see if any leads on the identity of Ramona had surfaced yet, but came to the unanimous agreement of returning to have a second shower and change clothes before doing so. The smell was too hard to shift, so bathing took priority.

Chapter Twenty-One

Smelling and feeling much better, Tessa and Lee still stalked into the Agency feeling decidedly crabby. The shocked stares at Tessa's bruised face only served to worsen her mood. Lady Marique looked over and moved to come and talk to Tessa, but a curt shake of Tessa's head dissuaded her. Leaving Lee in the foyer, Tessa headed to her pigeonhole to see if any information had been dropped off. There was a few hard copy forensics reports and a slim Agency file on one Ramona Taigue. Tessa grabbed the lot and took them to a spare desk to review.

As Tessa suspected here was nothing outside the usual in Tasha Lane's investigation and autopsy. The report could have literally been copied and pasted from the previous victims. The right hand was missing, there was a little spell bag hidden in her bra. The Agency file on Ramona was slightly more interesting. Apparently, she had not been "missed" by the Agency tests, but instead had proved to have incredibly weak skills, and was deemed to be not good enough to be an Agent. For one, she had miserably failed the psychological resilience tests. That ended her interactions with the Agency, so Tessa had to pursue other avenues.

Pulling out her phone, Tessa searched "Ramona Taigue Bayton" to see what the general internet had on her. There were a few very private social media files, featuring the beautiful red head in more sane days. She was most interested to see a website for a local occult store. It appeared that Ramona had been the owner of said store, listed as being one of the most successful businesses in Bayton. Excited, Tessa went to the contact page to see if the store was currently open, but it seemed that it had closed down fairly recently. She noted the details down anyway before returning to the search page.

She was about to read through a news article when she began to feel faint. Swooning, she checked the time on her phone and realised it was 3pm. She had not eaten since her morning coffee, and now her body had finally had enough of the abuse. Staggering to the returns box she threw in the file on Ramona, and tucked the lab reports into her bag to file later.

She rejoined Lee in the foyer, explaining how she felt. Surrendering the car keys to Lee, Tessa be grudgingly admitted that she could not drive in her state. He helped her to the car, put her in the passenger seat and drove them to a diner. The relief Tessa felt was palpable as she bit into her burrito, rolling her eyes in pleasure as she sat back against the booth seat.

"So, did you find out much?" Lee asked her when she had had a few mouthfuls and looked less pale.

"Mmm, yeah. Got a name and its definitely her. She was a pretty pathetic witch, so the Agency didn't pick her up, but she did own an occult store. Other than that, nothing new from forensics, the murder of Tasha was pretty standard for this case." Tessa stopped abruptly when she saw people at a nearby table stop mid-movement to be able to hear better. Awkwardly she took a few bites to let the silence settle. Lee picked up on her cue and changed the subject.

"Well, what are our plans for the evening?" he asked, trying to be subtle.

"I figure we should go to the market, see if our favourite seller is there. I might also try to ask Damien if he has any more details about our little problem. An address would be great, but I don't think he is going to be too happy to see me after everything. Considering that his brother is... involved, I might be able to get him to talk to me. It's worth a shot," she replied, reaching for her extra-large coffee.

"So, I take it we will pop over there in a few hours?"

"Yeah, for sure. They open at six, so we have a little time. What did you want to do?" Tessa asked, getting a cheeky glance in reply.

"Ohhh I don't know, I am sure we can entertain ourselves somehow," Lee said, rising to collect up their plates and carry them to the server. As much as Tessa was attracted to Lee, she just didn't feel up for any vigorous activity. When Lee returned, she said as much.

"That is totally fine! What would you feel better doing?" He asked, taking her hand in his, giving it a gentle rub. Tessa thought on it for a moment.

"Oh, I have an experience for you! But we have to go home for it!" she exclaimed in excitement. Lee was intrigued, wondering what new experience Tessa would introduce him to now. Her energy renewed, Tessa jumped up and trotted to the car, and Lee followed behind.

When they arrived home Tessa led him to the couch, making him sit down. He obliged and watched as she rustled around under the TV. Finally, she handed him a strange black device with buttons on it which he took carefully in his hands. Turning it back and forward, he looked confused. Tessa giggled and walked back to the TV, turning it on and fetching her own little black device. The TV lit up, and Tessa showed him a world of interactive heroes and villains, post-apocalyptic cities and monsters.

He was entranced, as ecstatic about this new experience as Tessa suspected he would be. Video gaming was unheard of in the 1950's, and the technology amazed him. When it came time to go to the markets, he was a little saddened to have to stop. Playing games with Tessa was a new favourite distraction for him. Still, they had to go, and Lee was seriously wondering if he could smuggle a gaming unit back to Hel. Unlikely, as much as it would make the stay far more tolerable. A power source was probably an issue, however.

The markets were busy this evening, with many people standing around talking earlier than usual. Little snippets of the conversations revealed that the murders were a hot topic amongst the locals. They swapped brutal detail with glee, and as soon as Tessa walked through, they all started staring and glaring. It was clear that most people blamed her, even those who she had previously considered to be friends. Trying to hold her head high, Tessa walked directly to her old stall, praying that Ramona would be there and she could finish this.

Luck was not with them tonight, and the stall stood deserted. No Ramona, no hag, nobody. Cursing under her breath, Tessa looked to Lee.

"OK, I will go talk to Damien. Please just... well just keep your distance, I want to keep him as calm as possible," she pleaded with him, knowing that Damien may lose control completely if he saw Lee, especially after the last time Damien had seen them.

"Of course. Please do not worry about me, I will be invisible," he promised, and quietly stepped away into the crowd. He even had his horns covered in a slouchy beanie today, so he was just an average guy.

Tessa headed over to the plain little door that led to Damien's rooms. Knocking on it gently, she waited to be admitted, preparing her speech to try and get in to even see the man himself. She rocked back and forward on her heels, nervous to be confronting the man she had loved, and hurt so badly. The door stood silent, so she knocked again. No answer.

Looking at the market around her, Tessa weighed up her options. Damien may just be doing his rounds, or he may be out on "business". Determined to find some answers, Tessa started to patrol the markets, moving quietly between the gathered people, searching for him. Finally, she chanced upon a stroke of luck, spotting Damien talking to one of the stall holders. She carefully made her way over, trying to remain unseen until she got close enough to plead her case.

Mr Big and Meaty from the door was the first to spot her, giving Lee a nudge and pointing her out. His face changed from genial to angered in a second.

"Leave now. Ye are banned from my turf. Ye ain't nothing to me now," he demanded, making the crowds around them scatter. Her heart skipped a beat, but Tessa held her position.

"I can't. I need your help with the investigation. I know who killed Adam," she pleaded, hoping to appeal to his need for revenge on his brother's killer.

"Don't care. Don't need to know-" Damien scowled, but Tessa interrupted him.

"Yes, you do. I know you care. I just need an address, anything about-" This time Tessa was interrupted as Damien pulled out his gun and pointed it at her. The crowd fell completely silent, all eyes on the drama before them. He swayed a little on the spot, trying to hold himself up with the air around him. It was clear to all that he was at least drunk, if not more.

"Look 'ere slut. 'Ear me right. I. AM. NOT. INTERESTED. Ye ain't got nuffin' for me. Nuffin' for some bitch who bin usin' me. Imma shoot ye and they ain't never findin' the body. Got it?" he slurred, taking off the safety as his heavy did the same. With two guns pointed at her and no card to play, Tessa took a sniffling breath, nodded and walked away. Praying she wouldn't be shot in the back Tessa ran from the market.

Lee met her halfway, having heard the sudden awed silence from the crowd. Seeing her running away crying, Lee was smart enough to simply join her in retreating to the car. When they had jumped in and locked the doors Tessa finally slowed her sobbing. Lee waited in silence for her to catch her breath.

"He pulled a freaking gun on me. Like, he properly pulled the gun and threatened me. Told me he would shoot me. Holy Hel I almost got shot. There is no way I am going back there, no matter what," she declared, genuinely afraid for her life for the second day in a row. This job was giving her anxiety.

"Want me to do something?" Lee asked and the ominous inflection in his voice was unmissable.

"No, let's just go home. We can look at the case again and review everything. There must be something."

As they drove back to the apartment Tessa's eye was caught by the bright light emanating from the moon. The fullness of the moon glared at her, providing a harsh reminder that tonight was likely the peak, and whatever mischief Ramona was up to was happening soon. She pointed it out to Lee wordlessly and her stress rose again. He sighed and drove faster.

Chapter Twenty-Two

Slamming the door open, Tessa and Lee got straight down to it. They spread out all the information they had over the apartment floor and desperately pored over it.

"Well, what do we know?" Lee asked, digging through the folder for all the lab reports before beginning to pace while reading them.

Tessa had a thought and began to scramble for her phone. She had completely forgotten about reading the news article she had seen earlier in the day and realised that it may contain something important. The tab was still open and she scanned the page quickly. Ramona Taigue had been in a car accident with her partner, Raven. He had died, and Ramona had sustained irreparable damage to her leg.

"Her partner died in a car accident? Could it be?" Tessa looked up, her eyes shining with inspiration.

"Witchy-bitch specifically mentioned love right?' Lee asked.

'Yep.'

"And she has a dead lover and... hey, do you have a street map of Bayton?' He had clearly had a thought, suddenly he stopped pacing and his eyes burned into hers. Tessa nodded dumbly, in awe of his intensity. She jumped up to fetch the map of Bayton pamphlet every new tenant got. Butterflies tore up her insides as she thought about confronting Ramona again.

"Don't worry, I will be by your side. We can do this," Lee said, his soulful eyes playing havoc with her heart.

"What? How did you? I didn't say anything, how did you know what I was worried about?" Tessa asked curiously.

'Well, I don't actually know... it was like I just got an impression of what you were thinking, or you were just kind of whispering in my mind. It was really odd.' Lee had a slight fear in his eyes, but Tessa could not place why. He soon stifled it dutifully.

'Has it happened before? Could it be because my blood raised you?' queried Tessa, but Lee shook his head.

'Never happened with any other witch. I didn't think it worked that way,' he replied idly, once again absently scratching his horns as he thought. Shyly, Tessa finally piped up on her idea.

'Well could it be from the... you know... soul sex?' She started blushing wildly at the mere mention of it. Lee grinned at the memory but nodded sagely.

'You know, ever since we experienced that I have felt something was different. I think you're right. But as much as I hate to interrupt such an important conversation, it is however keeping us from getting revenge on that bitch for messing your face up... and the murders of course.' It was Tessa's turn to nod curtly before she turned away again to fetch her map. They spread it out on the floor and Lee grabbed a marker.

'So the first murder was here in North Bayton wasn't it? This lane according to your notes, while the second was south... here, yes?' Tessa nodded, not wanting to break his stride. 'Next was the Bayton East ones, here and here, but it was only the second one that counted right? Then the one last night was here, way up west... oh!' Lee exclaimed, drawing a line between the north and south murders, then the east and west murders. Dead centre, X marking the spot, was Bayton cemetery. They looked at each other excitedly before Tessa broke the stand-off.

'She said that it would take a long time to prepare for what I am guessing will be a ritual. It must be there. I vote we prepare ourselves. Let's haul ass, make some more green powder vial bombs and not go in half cocked. I am sure she will have some undead protection there.' Lee agreed wholeheartedly and they busied themselves with selecting herbs, grinding up ingredients and filling their precious little vials.

They spoke very little, focusing intently on the task at hand.

At least this way we can avoid all the talk of feelings, Tessa mused, glad that avoidance was their unspoken agreement. Tessa even modified a belt to be able to hold vials like a bandolier, so they were ready to go when she needed them. When she had strapped her belt on, hidden a knife in her boot and had her Agency issue laser on her hip, she felt pretty badass. She preferred not to use the sleek little laser, but it really didn't hurt to carry it. Her magick deadening handcuffs went into her kit too.

From somewhere Lee produced a laser also making Tessa raise an eyebrow, considering it was illegal for civilians to carry one. He simply shrugged with a cheeky look on his face.

'Borrowed it from one of your lovely co-workers when we were patrolling.'

'Borrowed? Nobody gives away their laser, they would get fired and then arrested. So, you borrowed it huh?' Her voice held a great deal of mock accusation. It didn't really bother her where he had gotten it from, right now she had a feeling that they would need the extra firepower.

'Hey, if your so-called Agents are so careless as to just leave it lying in the car with the window open, they deserve what they get. Mine now,' he finished cheekily, grinning away at his mischief.

Tessa just sighed, finding it highly unlikely an Agent would leave their laser out in the open. Still, his cheekiness was so endearing, and she wished she could just spend a night in bed with him again. That time they spent just curling up, talking and connecting had been something so sacred. The sex was just a bonus of course.

Lee must have caught that thought as he began to grin like the proverbial Cheshire Cat. Tessa blushed again, deciding there was definite downsides to having to spend the night hunting a crazy witch. At the same moment she felt a shudder of nerves run through her, reminding herself again that soon Lee would be gone. She already didn't want him to go, having gotten used to his company both in and out of the bed.

Shaking off those thoughts Tessa rechecked all of her supplies, adding a canister of salt in case there was a spell to be stopping. Given that Ramona may be raising a dead lover, Tessa was pretty sure she would need to void a spell, just in case they arrived too late. She also called in to Sir McAdams to let him know of her hunch, and he wholeheartedly approved. He gave her an emergency number to dial if needed and arranged to have another few Agents patrolling the area to be close at hand should her hunch prove correct. All kitted out and ready to go, Tessa and Lee looked at each other, nodded and headed to the door. It was time for the Reckoning of Ramona.

Chapter Twenty-Three

The drive over to the cemetery was short and relatively quiet, the only noise was the careful rustling as both of them nervously checked their supplies again and again. Tessa had grabbed a spare knife which was made of iron, as well as one of silver, just in case she needed something with a little more kick to break the spell. Lee had somehow acquired some mysterious daggers of his own, with a serpentine blade and demonic heads forged into the hilts. When asked he merely shrugged.

'Need something to do in Hel. Took some iron with me. Combined it with ash of a demon, as well as a bone handle. I made them to honour a lost friend, and they are still my companions. Useful for helping cute witches and stopping the evil ones if needed,' he responded, tension over the situation not allowing his full bright smile to show through. Tessa just nodded and let the car lapse back into silence. Now was not the time for idle banter, nor tales of friends long lost.

They parked a street back from the cemetery and silently walked over. Hoping for the element of surprise, they squeezed through a barely open gate and began to search the deserted cemetery. The cemetery in Bayton was huge, having once included a church and many satellite buildings, however most religion was abandoned when the witch trials revealed the presence of witches, demons and a whole host of other critters. The church just couldn't compete when fae and nymphs flittered through suburban streets and fashion catwalks.

Eventually the citizens had pulled down what remained of those buildings in order to fit more dead in the overcrowded cemetery. Now

Bayton had the dubious honour of being home to the largest inner-city cemetery worldwide. It also happened to be full of both official and unofficial burials. There were rows upon rows of grave markers, as well as dubious mounds of dirt waiting to trip the unwary visitor. As much as Tessa was loathe to use any kind of light, tripping thrice on the rough burial mounds and once on something she suspected was an exposed limb forced her to summon a muted witch light. Even at the full moon, the moonlight was not enough to penetrate a Bayton cemetery.

Its gentle glow fell over the graves, giving an eerie feel. As much as Tessa knew that any ghosts hanging around could be dealt with swiftly with a single spell or a silvery stab, the effect was still creepy. Tessa was more afraid of interrupting one of the impromptu burials than ghosts. That would involve guns.

Luckily very few people seemed to want to wander around the cemetery on this night. After almost an hour of searching, Tessa realised why. There was a pall of negativity over the area, an itching kind of toxicity that made people want to leave immediately, even if they did not know why. It had to be the work of someone acquainted to magick, and on a hunch, Tessa followed the feeling.

Over a small crest they finally saw what they were looking for. A tiny light flickering from a tiny fire, almost hidden between the head stones. Tessa looked to Lee and they silently quickened their pace, picking carefully through the graves. As she doused her magickal light, Tessa begged the Earth Mother that there be no open graves for them to fall into. Falling into a grave only days after being abducted to the sewer might just be the bitter end of Tessa's sanity. It seemed their luck held and soon they were on the very edge of the light the fire threw off.

Ramona's crimson hair glinted in the fire light as she busied herself around a grave that she had clearly spent the day digging up. There was an abandoned shovel beside a massive pile of dirt that had merely been tossed over all the nearby graves. She had lined up little packets of herbs next to the fire and seemed to be working from a well-used writing pad, the pages torn and curling.

The severed hands had been lined up, all pointing towards the grave. They were directing the energy emanating from Ramona and the murder locations. She kept casting the grave loving stares and even gently caressed the headstone, clearly deep in her madness. He had to be reasonably fresh if the stench was anything to go by.

Ramona had her back to them as she consulted her book, so Tessa took her chance. So far, they had seen no zombies, so she stealthily moved forward to deal with the woman herself. Grabbing the shovel on the way, Tessa had it raised and swinging by the time Ramona noticed she was not alone.

'You b-' Her words were lost in the sickening crunch as the shovel connected with her face, knocking her back and almost into the grave.

'Payback's a bitch and so am I!' shouted Tessa, gloating slightly as she thought of her own bruised and broken face.

Ramona glared through the blood flowing freely from her nose and muttered some arcane incantation. Tessa warily watched the grave, but the shuffling and murmuring came from further down the hill. Clearly, she had back up hidden away down there. Of course, Ramona had been ultra prepared.

Lee chose that moment to appear, leaping from between the graves to stand before them, twin daggers in hand.

'I will deal with this; you thump the girl. Wouldn't be right if I did it and all,' he shouted back to Tessa, who almost swooned at the sight. A demon with fire in his eyes and wicked daggers in his hands was quite the sight. Distracted, Tessa watched as he threw his first powder vial. Ramona took her chance to throw herself at Tessa. Catching her around the hips, Tessa yelped in surprise as she went down hard. She thanked her lucky stars that she was wearing thick jeans as the vials on the back of her belt shattered, spreading glass and green powder everywhere.

Ramona simply grinned up at her, drawing herself up like a demented cobra prepared to strike. She remained in a position straddling Tessa as she began to do a little dance in the firelight.

'I may actually enjoy killing you. You just had to be so contrary didn't you little Mary?' Ramona spoke in a sing song manner, grabbing a sharp athame from her discarded bag. The blade gleamed in the light, lush garnets set into the hilt glinting blood red, a promise of the magick it was made for. Tessa drew her own knife from her boot, not willing to be another victim of that evil knife and its equally evil owner. It had clearly been fed many previous victims.

Ramona swiped at her, missing her face by mere millimetres. Tessa ducked to the side before bucking the other witch off and jumping up. Still mildly dazed Ramona scrambled up, weaving back and forth. Tessa could draw her laser now that Ramona was off her, clicking it onto stun only.

'That's cheating,' whined Ramona, drawing some kind of powder from a hidden source in her dress. Tessa ducked away as she threw it, but some still landed on her jeans leg. She glanced down, waiting for something to happen, but the powder seemed to have no reaction. Tessa grinned and pointed the laser at Ramona, keen to finish this.

Short of looking worried, Ramona merely began muttering under her breath, as calm as can be. Tessa sighed and fired a shot, but it went wide as her leg collapsed. She fell to the floor, realising she could no longer feel her limb. Ramona cackled and began to advance as Tessa scrabbled in her bag for her salt. She fired another shot but it went through Ramona's hair, singeing a few locks on the way through. Finally, she managed to find the container of salt and dumped the entire thing over her leg. She felt the spell break, but her lower leg remained motionless. Ramona grinned wildly as Tessa cursed under her breath.

'You like that? Little creation of my own, but don't worry, your leg will work again. Too bad it will just give me the time I need to finish you,' with that she leapt, swinging wildly and knocking the laser from Tessa's hand. While Tessa did try to throw herself to the side, there was no avoiding this one. The knife gashed a deep line along the side of her ribs, making her cry out in pain. The gems on the hilt seemed to glow in the light as the knife went up in another arc. When it came down and Tessa successfully dodged it, she saw that the gems were indeed incandescent.

Interesting.

She would have to investigate that one when the knife wasn't being used to kill her. She bucked and rolled, dislodging Ramona and ending up on top of her. Far from discouraged Ramona kept slashing, but Tessa finally had the upper hand. Using the hilt of her own knife she smashed the other woman in the face before trying to wrestle the twisted athame out of Ramona's hands.

Realising what was happening, Ramona began to scream and cuss, grabbing Tessa by the clothes and trying to head butt her. They rolled again, Ramona writhing wildly and clawing at Tessa's arms while Tessa went for the blade. When they came to a stop Tessa was bruised and bloody, but Ramona had her own knife in her side.

The glow from the gems in the hilt lit up the night as Ramona scrabbled uselessly at it, but the fire in her eyes soon died out. She looked to Tessa.

'Just. Wanted him. You. Bitch. One day. You will lose. Him too,' she gasped as she collapsed into the dirt from the grave, dying beside her lover. Ramona had even reached out to attempt to touch the headstone.

'You just had to get the last word,' remarked Tessa, feeling callous about slinging sarcasm at a dead woman. A little cattiness seemed justified. Holding her side tenderly, Tessa retrieved her laser and looked to see how Lee was faring. He had a bite or two, but was doing well, a swathe of re-dead zombies now littered the floor and only a handful remained. Tessa flicked her laser to kill and picked the last of them off for him. He looked around for a moment in confusion, before jogging over.

'Hey, that's cheating, I was having fun there. How's the... oh! What happened to your side? I'll kill her!' he spoke too quickly, still high on the adrenaline from the fight. Tessa laughed dejectedly, despite the pain in her ribs that the effort caused. She started to feel odd, as if the world was going in slow motion, but she still couldn't keep up.

'Way ahead of you there, boy.' she attempted bravado, showing him the body of Ramona. Her madness still tainted the air after death. The garnets in the hilt of the knife were still faintly glowing. It was as if the knife was ensuring it took every last flicker of life.

'Woah... I had heard of knives with bits that glow when they got bloodied, but have never seen one. Apparently they... Tess!' he cried out as she slumped to the floor, unconscious.

Chapter Twenty-four

Tessa awoke in her own room, cuddled up in bed with all her warmest bedding. She almost forgot what had happened until her side began to ache with the movement of breathing alone. She felt completely disoriented, unsure of the time or day. It appeared to be bright out, but that could always just be a rogue streetlight in Bayton. Grimacing, she began to sit up, but Lee came bolting over, having just appeared in the doorway.

'Stay there you! I swear you are the worst patient possible, you thumped the poor doctor who tried to patch you up. Twice. I ended up having to do it.' Tessa just looked at him incredulously.

'They let you stay? They didn't send you back?'

'Well initially I had to let them know what happened, then they needed someone to look after you. Apparently you have no family, so they let me stay until you are better!' he answered, smiling benevolently like he was Mother freaking Theresa for looking after her. He was far too perky for how her head felt. She groaned loudly, the pain in her head and side competing for attention. Lee shoved some kind of tea into her hands.

'Here, this will make it better,' he explained, but Tessa looked at him dubiously. She was always unwilling to touch an odd smelling brew. He sighed dramatically as she giggled.

'Can't I have some kind of pill?' She was wrinkling her nose at the smell like a displeased cat. Lee gave a look of feigned offence but snorted in laughter.

'Uh no. Now drink it.' Tessa complied, soon finding that those weird herbs could be very effective. Again. One day she would learn to trust Lee's blends. Tessa caught that thought sadly, remembering their situation and why he was here.

'So, what happened? Did everything work out?' she asked Lee, worried about what happened after she fell unconscious.

'Yup, it all got worked out, everything got tied up with a nice little bow. Witch Bitch is dead, the zombies are all sorted out and buried again and the lover remains dead.' Lee caught her up as he sat down on the bed. He had an oddly mischievous look on his face, like a kid trying to hide a stolen candy.

'OK, I guess that's good. What are you looking so... mysterious about?' Tessa asked, feeling innately suspicious. The grin on Lee's face widened conspiratorially as he got up to pull something wrapped in cloth from his bag. He carefully pulled back the fabric to reveal Ramona's athame.

'Lee! You took that? You stole evidence. Not only that, you stole it from a dead murderer's body! I am so going to get fired, and worse! How could you? Why?' Freaking out, Tessa was beginning to shout. Lee held up a hand in an attempt to calm her. She was going to split her stitches with this much excitement.

'Now, now, I am just righting a wrong. This is not of this earth. This is a demonblade, made in Hel by one of the more powerful demons. It should not be here, nor should it be wielded by a human. I am obligated to return it to Hel now I know of its existence,' he said, calmly but earnestly. Tessa pursed her lips, unhappy at the whole situation.

'Sure, so you are *only* going to return it to Hel?' Tessa was not buying it for second.

'Well, nothing says I can't study it a little first. I mean, I have a bit more time before I and it needs to be returned,' Lee explained, having the decency to look at least a little ashamed of his behaviour. Just enough to seem on the good side still.

'But what in Hel did the Agency say when the weapon I used to kill Ramona suddenly went missing?' Tessa admonished Lee, who grinned wider than ever.

'That's the best part, I replaced it!'

'With what?' snapped Tessa.

'Oh, just a very similar knife, same shape, same size. It looked very appropriate, and they never asked any more after I described the fight to them. Everything fit rather nicely,' Lee finished, sitting back on the bed and looking very pleased with himself. Again, Tessa was reminded how much demons were like cats.

She sighed, rubbing her head in defeat. There really wasn't much she could do about it, unless she wanted to report Lee and deal with the repercussions. It was probably best that the demonblade was returned to Hel, rather than stay in this world to be exploited repeatedly, either by the Agency or a crazed witch serial killer. She really didn't want to know what else the creepy blade might be capable of.

'Fine, I guess. Take it back and do whatever with it, I don't want to know about it,' she grumbled as Lee nodded enthusiastically.

'Oh sure, uh huh, not a problem,' he agreed, eyes gleaming as he scurried off to start studying the infernal blade. Tessa couldn't help but both laugh and sigh again in frustration. She would definitely miss his antics, and his fascination with absolutely everything. He had such a passion for living and discovering new experiences. Tessa couldn't help but think that she had never met anyone like him and may never again. The thought made her ache more than her physical wounds.

Sir McAdams came to debrief Tessa shortly after, as Lee was duty bound to notify him as soon as she was up. It appeared that the two had gotten well acquainted in the aftermath. The Sir glanced around her apartment with a clear distaste, but it was quickly masked.

'Well Lady Bale, what a case! The clean-up was... extensive. Not that you aren't to be commended for all your work of course. All the appropriate reports have been done by your demon and myself. I...

uhhhh... just need your signature to file them all.' He said, pushing a wad of documents toward her. Tessa looked to Lee to verify the contents of the documents. She couldn't be bothered reading them all now. He nodded slowly, so Tessa signed the various forms with a still shaking hand. With that Sir McAdams brusquely shuffled the papers together and packed them into his briefcase. Tessa had one more question to ask him.

"Did we ever find out where the Hel she got all the zombies from? I mean she had to buy a shovel to dig up her partner, so I am guessing she got the others above ground."

"Yes, we certainly did. Turns out initially she dug her own. Eventually she got fed up with that so she seduced some miserable sap at a funeral home and had gotten her hands on his keys. Well, we actually suspect he gave them to her for some late night liaisons. Yes, in the funeral home." Sir McAdams spoke with clear disgust. Tessa looked a little shocked and could not think of a single thing to say. Her boss took this chance to make a break for it and awkwardly nodded a farewell. He was clearly relieved to leave her cramped apartment, wincing as he went through the doorway that still bore dark blood stains and hole from the curse tongue.

Tessa looked to Lee and sighed loudly. After a brief check over by the doctor it was finally over. She was tattered and bruised, but it was over, to Hel with their "extensive clean-up".

She spent her well-earned recuperation days sleeping and chatting to Lee, until her side had healed to a neat scar. They often played video games much to Lee's delight, and he quickly worked his way through several titles. He discovered how good it was to play co-operatively with his lover. After Tessa had recovered more physically, many of their gaming sessions evolved into more of a sensual moment.

The luxury of long days spent in bed entwined with Lee and not having to worry about where her next payment was going to come from was enchanting to Tessa. Being on respite was fully paid by the Agency, as so many Agents got into scrapes on the job. Being a full-blooded Agent was amazing, well worth the internship. She often found herself happily looking at Lee during these days. A glance at the source of her new joy. But it was so tainted.

The ache in her heart was an unsaid thing, a ghost haunting every moment of bliss they experienced. Neither was willing to discuss the depth of their feelings, nor that this utopia had to end.

Eventually, the day came.

The reports had all been filed, her bonus pay had hit her account and all families notified. This marked the time that Lee had to go, his permitted time to be here at an end. Tessa arranged for the banishing ceremony to be done in a nearby forest as it often involved far greater plumes of sulphur and dramatic noises than the summoning. Her neighbours could put up with a lot, but not that.

The day that Lee would finally be sent back to Hel dawned as any other in Bayton at this time of year, cold and foggy. They had spent the night curled up together, whispering small things to each other in the early hours until their voices cracked from exhaustion. It wasn't even about sex.

They enjoyed a last coffee together in the morning, yawning away and shuffling around the small apartment. Each dressed quietly, secretly trying to look their best. Tessa treated them to a sumptuous lunch with some of her bonus pay.

It almost felt like a ritual, the send-off for a lover to an interstate trip, however the lover would never be able to return in this case. Tessa could spend the rest of her life summoning new demons, but she would never find him again. The summoning process was like a lottery, completely random with very slim chances of winning.

The restaurant they finally settled on was a sweet little Italian place, a beautiful cliché of Italian dining. There was plastic olive trees, checked table cloths with paper over them and framed portraits of dignified family members. The small talk around the décor sustained them for the start of the meal, but it soon ground to a halt before they had even finished their garlic bread.

Their main meals cooled as Tessa and Lee sat and stared, both unable to articulate anything particularly coherent. Tessa picked at her salad, wondering why on earth she had chosen it in the first place.

Was she really that distracted by these events that she thought lettuce was a good idea?

She turned to pick at the pasta instead. Clearing her throat awkwardly, Tessa attempted speech.

'So what is Hel like? To go back there?' she asked, shoving a forkful of spaghetti into her mouth in a show of normalcy.

'Well it's... interesting. It's mostly just nothingness, a big black expanse. But it isn't bad. It is just all of us existing there. We can talk, organise, create things, well the demons can, the humans mostly just bop around and learn things. Sometimes they get popped in a new body and get out for a lifetime. It is pretty strange when you are used to, this,' Lee replied, gesturing around the diner. 'When brand new souls come in, they are usually pretty scared, but they find their blood and binding ties relatively quickly. That settles them down pretty quickly. The human souls definitely seem to avoid the demons in general though. I suppose the stigma remains in the afterlife.' Tessa nodded slowly.

'So, you aren't... lonely?'

'Oh, not really, I mean everyone can socialise. Most people stick with their partners if they had a hand-fasting ceremony, the binding I mentioned in life, if not most return to their family. But new souls occasionally meet and get to know each other. Demons aren't all that social, I guess,' he trailed off, lost in thought. It wasn't an unpleasant journey, and yet Lee was filled with trepidation.

Tessa considered his words carefully, mulling over what the afterlife was looking like. She was happy that Lee would have others around him, but it still tore her up inside. The insight into the afterlife was a small relief to her though, for her own end. It was rare that people got this kind of chance. Mostly it was a matter of faith, and that was tenuous at best.

Feeling far too melancholy, Tessa checked her phone. Finally, the appointed hour had come.

Chapter Twenty-Five

They silently trudged to the open rock bank that the Agency kept for the banishings, Tessa's bag bulging with the supplies needed. They also set up in silence, Tessa laying out the protection circle while Lee sulked and glared at various inanimate objects. Even a wayward critter running into the circle received the glare.

They stood face to face, Lee inside the circle and Tessa on the outer, trying to hold it together. She opened and closed her mouth, wanting to say exactly the right words for the situation but finding none. Something pragmatic, or insightful would have been great in this moment. Anything at all. Lee simply scratched at his horns and shrugged, not wanting to open his mouth and betray his deep emotions. They stood like that for a few seconds before Tessa coughed and finally decided what to say, although it all sounded like pitiful platitudes in the face of her true emotions.

'Well, you saved my life a few times. I know that is why demons are called forth and all but thank you. I can't even put into words how grateful I am... and... I really enjoyed the time we had. I really will miss having you around and the experiences we had.'

With her flood of awkward words, the memories came back too, the moment their souls connected, the feeling of being in his arms, her tentatively touching his horns for the first time. She choked up and could speak no more, finally allowing her silent tears to fall down her face. Lee bit his lip and nodded stoically, keeping back his own tears, as was his duty. He had to go back and that was that, demons did not belong in this world. He bowed silently and stepped into the very centre of the circle.

Tessa took up her place at the top of the circle, opening her spell book to where she had scribbled Lee's personal banishing spell. She began to chant unsteadily as she built her fire, throwing in the generic banishing herbs. Her voice cracked, giving way again to little gulping sobs. She was forced to stop and clear her throat before starting anew, more tears freely running down her face as the circle began to glow. The stench of sulphur began to taint the air. Her chest ached as though her heart was breaking. As always, she buried her personal feelings and kept on with her duty.

The murky ether rose and began to obscure her view of Lee. It was a blackness, like a billowing fog. A little taste of Hel, a frigid wind whipped up to join it. He looked up sorrowfully as the he began to lose sight of her, the cold of Hel beginning to surround him and infuse his bones. Their eyes met and in that second, each knew the depth of what the other felt. Honour and duty were taking it all from them now.

The smoky tendrils swirled higher around Lee and he was completely out of sight. A life without him close by thundered through Tessa's mind. A life that now felt as though it was rendered meaningless. What would she do? Find a human male and settle down? Live without the most interesting person she had ever met, someone who truly inspired and fascinated her? In the last few weeks she had truly felt alive, rather than just existing. Prior to now her only goal was to be an Agency witch just to piss off her parents. No longer was she trying to avoid getting attached to anyone because of what she was running from, or to.

With that revelation she threw her book aside and bolted into the circle. She ran for the centre of the ether and dove into it, praying both that he would still be there and that she wouldn't be taken to Hel by mistake. For long, agonising seconds she fell, finding only air. Fear rose in her gut. Then she found him, beautiful hard flesh. The force of her tackle pushed both of them out of the salt circle, both of them landing in a crying and hugging heap. Neither noticed the pain, bumps or scratches from landing on the rough granite. They were too caught up in the ecstasy and apprehension.

'Do you know what you have done?' asked Lee incredulously, holding her face in his shaking hands.

'Yes. And I would do it again,' Tessa replied kissing him deeply as tears continued to fall, tears of joy, tears of fear, tears of uncertainty.

'I love you.'

IF YOU HAVE ENJOYED this book, please consider giving a good review on Amazon or GoodReads. To authors, especially indie ones like me, it makes a huge difference. Word of mouth is also very important!

IF YOU WISH TO JOIN my ARC reader team or mailing list, please email me at Ysadora.alexander.author@gmail.com or on any of the usual social media sites at Ysadora Writes. You will know me by the lil' witch!

DEMON HUNTED, BOOK Two of The Bayton Agency is coming in Q2 2025.

FAETALITY, BOOK ONE of The Bayton Fae is coming late 2025.

www.ingramcontent.com/pod-product-compliance
Lightning Source LLC
Chambersburg PA
CBHW022021170626
46808CB00003B/1006